The Wrong Cake

and other stories

Sarah Boyd

Published by Minster & Grey
Copyright © Sarah Boyd 2019

ISBN 978-1-913036-68-3

Cover design by Ravina Patel

To my father, champion book devourer

CONTENTS

Intruder..7

Shopping Trip...23

Desperate Measures 35

Full Up 45

Change of Scene 59

Dorothy Daunt 75

Coming Home 91

Wendover Street...101

Memories...119

The Wrong Cake 135

Fancy That...143

Wonder Vision 153

Pretty Ordinary...169

Revenge..181

The Crossing..197

Lasting Legacy...209

Finders Keepers 225

INTRUDER

The dog is my cover story. People don't ask what you're doing if you have a dog with you. They talk to you, of course – more than if you're on your own. I'm prepared for that. They trust you. Well, maybe not if you have a particularly fierce-looking dog or one with a muzzle on. But mine looks the furthest from fierce you could imagine.

They'll ask what breed the dog is, how old and (if there's a child with them), whether it's a boy or a girl dog, and whether it's friendly. They'll let me know (if they are walking a dog themselves), whether there's a dog further up the road that needs careful watching in case it should decide to attack mine. Whether it's 'frisky' or not, and will go for anything that moves. Sometimes, they'll give me a whole catalogue of their dog's latest procedures at the vet, accompanied by the costs, with much eye-rolling, eyebrow-raising and sighing.

Frankly, I couldn't care less about other people's dogs, and what they fork out at the vet is their business. That's what insurance is for. Otto is no trouble, most of the time anyway. If another dog wants to do more than sniff his behind, I just scoop him up and tuck him under my arm. You get used to doing that with dachshunds, anyway. When I first had him, I'd let him off the lead a lot. Seemed kinder. But then, of course, with his little legs, I'd lose him in the park's long grass and I used to feel like a right berk when I had to yell, 'Otto!' countless times to try and get him back. So now the lead stays on most of the time.

My mates ask me if I feel silly being seen with such a small dog, as I am well built and look like a labourer, standing six foot two in my socks. Well, I won't deny it felt a bit funny at first – I don't mind telling you that I *was* a little embarrassed when I set off with Otto on our first trip, just to the corner shop to pick up the paper. Jan had persuaded me that we needed to buy a pet and then she set her heart on a flaming sausage dog when I would have been more than happy with a retriever, or something a bit… well, bigger.

After we'd had him a few weeks, though, I noticed just how many other men out there are walking dinky-sized dogs. Pugs with their wrinkly faces, French bulldogs with their sticking up ears, and a few other dachshunds, too. So no, I don't feel silly at all these days. Besides, you can go out any time of the day or night with a dog, and people don't bat an eyelid. It can be 11 o'clock at night and I'll say to Jan, 'I'll just take the dog out for his late night final.'

'OK,' she says to me, 'When this programme's finished I'm turning in. Can you lock up?' And that's it. By the time I get back – it could be in half an hour, could be two, depending on how business goes – I know she'll be asleep, gently snoring, flat on her back as usual, with no clue as to where I've gone. And Otto won't tell, will he?

It's an ideal situation in many ways. She has her own life – still working in the charity shop two days a week, and helping out in the school library – and I have mine. Two years ago, I officially retired, although I still do small bits of work for friends. Just odd jobs mainly – fixing fences, sorting out dripping taps – and I get paid in cash, naturally. And then I still help out at my old workplace once a week if they need me. The 'oldest Saturday boy ever' as I joke with the teenagers there.

The rest of the time? Well, I can do what I like, more or less. Jan has plenty of friends and she spends a lot of time with her sister, who only lives around the corner. Half the time, I think she just wants to get away from me, to be honest. That's OK – the feeling's mutual.

There's football on Saturdays – watching not playing. I just support the local team. If it's a home game, I'll watch with Ian, if he's around, and we'll go for a few pints after the match to celebrate or drown our sorrows, as the case may be. There will always be someone I know in the pub.

Then there's my fishing – I can set off early in the morning and not return until it's getting dark. It's the solitude I like most of all. I'm not bothered about how many carp I catch. Of course, I'll tell Jan that I'm off to fish and set off with all my equipment, but sometimes, I'll be somewhere else altogether, which explains why I come back empty-handed on occasion. I'm sure she thinks that I'm just a rubbish fisherman, but I don't care.

It's not a secret existence exactly, just, well... I prefer it if Jan doesn't know about every aspect of my life. There's no need. I'm sure she has secrets of her own, although maybe not as big as mine...

Anyway, today I was at my mate Ted's house. He wants me to help dig a pond in his back garden, which is a pretty big one for around here. I think it's a bad idea, personally. He has two young grandchildren who come over every Saturday, so it'll have to have a grille fitted over the top, which won't look very attractive. Then, someone will have to watch like a hawk every time the kiddies come round and no one will be able to relax. And he says he wants giant koi in there as well, but I don't think he realises just how much it costs to stock a pond properly. Then all it takes is one determined heron and he could have lost hundreds of pounds. Still, he's paying me a decent amount of cash so I won't open my mouth.

My friend came to greet me. 'Werner,' he said.

It's my name. What can I say? German name, German dog, although more by accident than design, seeing as how Jan chose the dog.

'Ted.'

'How's it going?'

'Fine, fine.'

'About the pond. I thought we could put it over there. What do you think?'

Overhanging tree branches, I think to myself. *He's going to be fishing leaves out of it all winter.*

'Fine, fine. All I need is a shovel, then I can get started.'

My friend, who's surely aged more than I have in the thirty years or so since I've known him, went off in the direction of his shed. Halfway there, he turned and looked at me over his shoulder. 'Oh yes, that's what

I wanted to tell you. Did you hear what happened the other day? To Geoff?

Now, Geoff is in my group of friends, but on the fringes, if you like. I don't know him that well. We support different teams and he drinks in different pubs. I've never cared for him, to be honest, although some of my mates are on quite friendly terms. I haven't had much to do with him – at least not until two weeks ago.

I'd been 'walking the dog' one night. Only I wasn't, actually. Otto was safely tied up and he's always been a quiet dog. If you leave him for an hour he won't bark for his master to come back, he'll just lie down and wait patiently for me. This has served me well on several occasions. I'm not worried about anyone nicking him – I'm sure he'd nip their ankle if they tried.

Anyway, this particular evening, I had a lot of business to do and it was already dark – but not dark enough, as it turned out. It was getting late and had just started to drizzle. As I turned the corner to set off back for home, who should come strolling along but Geoff. He'd almost caught me out, but not quite. Luckily, I'd just untied Otto from the alleyway so my cover story was trotting along happily by my side.

'Evening, Werner.'

'Geoff.'

'Wasn't expecting you here.'

'Well, you know, just walking the dog.' I indicated Otto with my hand, in case he hadn't looked that far down.

'Ah yes, the famous sausage dog. Funny little bugger, isn't he? I prefer bigger breeds myself.' He gave me a searching look under the streetlight. 'Bit late for a walk, isn't it? In this weather? Shouldn't you be watching telly with the missus?'

I gave an approximation of a laugh. 'I could say the same of you. Just popped out to the shop for a chocolate bar.'

'It's closed.'

'Yes, so it is. It must be later than I thought. Got carried away watching the film.'

'Oh, what film was that?'

'Something on DVD. I forget the title now. It wasn't that good anyway. Well, got to be getting back. I'll be seeing you.'

'Night, Werner.' He put the stress on the first word, as if it was significant that we were meeting at such a late hour. Then, he was off, striding into the night down a side road.

Did he live around here then? I could have sworn he lived on the other side of town but now I wasn't so sure. Maybe he'd moved. I hoped not. It would make things very... *difficult* if I started running into Geoff on my nocturnal outings. Very tricky indeed.

It unsettled me, seeing him. So much so that I couldn't stop mulling it over the next day, and for the whole of that week his face kept returning to me at inopportune moments. What had *he* been doing that night, come to think of it? Did he have similar interests to my own?

'About Geoff.' Ted had now returned with the shovel and a wheelbarrow. 'Last Sunday it was.'

'Oh yes?' I replied, breaking through the turf with the first swing of the hefty shovel. I'm still strong, even though I'm collecting my pension.

* * *

Geoff's story

As I said to the police on Sunday, I've absolutely no idea how it happened. A complete mystery. There I was, in the bathroom first thing, doing my morning shave, as I do every day, when I caught a movement out of the corner of my eye. We get huge spiders in this old house so I thought maybe it was that. I don't mind them but Bel goes potty if she sees one. In fact, she's terrified of practically any creature that makes sudden movements, come to think of it.

Now, I'd taken my glasses off to shave, as is my usual practice, so I just carried on with the razor until I'd finished. I don't like anything interfering with my routine, see. But just as I was about to put them back on, there was another movement. Something told me this was no spider. As soon as I'd towelled my face and could see properly, I turned around fully and saw it. I couldn't believe my eyes at first, but there it was, slithering slowly along – *there was a snake in my bathroom*! It was gradually emerging from behind the roll top bath, gliding soundlessly over the tiled floor, its head shifting from side to side.

It wasn't a small adder type of snake that you might be unlucky enough to find in the grass while out walking – though that would have been bad enough. No. This thing must have been about five feet long, thicker than your arm. It was looking straight at me now, flicking its tongue in and out. I was rooted to the spot – I didn't want to provoke it. What were you supposed to do with snakes? Stay still? Run like hell? It was keeping to the edge of the room, heading for the toilet bowl, where it started coiling itself around the base.

Well, I was terrified, I don't mind telling you. I reckoned there was enough distance between me and the creature for me to make it safely to the door. When we had our house extended, I'd told Bel the bathroom was too large but I was grateful for its capaciousness now. So I fled out of the room and slammed the door, then roared down to Bel, who was baking in the kitchen, to call the police.

She couldn't make out what I was saying so I had to run downstairs and explain, then run back upstairs in case the thing escaped under the door. I opened the door gingerly, just enough to see if it was still there. It was fully coiled around the toilet now, looking at me with an unblinking stare. I found my breathing had become shallow and rapid. Half of me couldn't bear to look at it, the other half was mesmerized. Then, as I was watching, it seemed to be uncoiling itself slowly. God! It was coming to get me!

Now, spiders I can deal with, no problem. Snakes are a different story. I've always been a bit scared of them, with their scaly bodies and forked tongues, and face to face, as it were, this one was horrible – huge and scaly with black and orange splodges along its back. There are no zoos around here so it must have been an escaped pet – though how anyone could want to share their living space with a monster like that, goodness only knows.

My next worry was – when I could stop thinking about it coiling around my neck and suffocating me – how could I prevent it from sliding out under the door? There's a gap of almost an inch. I've been meaning to do something about it for ages, the draughts in winter are terrible, and although its body looked too thick to pass through, I had no idea whether snakes could slim themselves down enough to fit through small spaces (like cats, but to a more extreme extent). Presumably, they can, else how on earth could this one have got into my bathroom?

So I wrenched a towel out of the linen cupboard on the landing and quickly stuffed it into the gap, hoping that would be enough to contain it. Bel, meanwhile, now that she knew what was lurking in her own bathroom, was on the phone to the police, hysterical, and by the sounds of it, having trouble trying to make herself understood. She's petrified of all reptiles you see, but then I defy anyone *not* to be terrified if they encounter a snake in their own home.

Having blocked the gap as best I could, I ran downstairs and together we sat in the lounge on the sofa, pressed close together, waiting for the police to arrive.

'What are we going to do?' My wife was shrieking now, clutching her cheeks. 'I can't go up there. I can't! Don't leave me alone down here, Geoff, *don't leave me!*'

Bel pulled me back down onto the sofa in a panic. I was only going to check for the police car. Thank goodness it wasn't our turn to have the grandkids that weekend. After 15 long minutes, a squad car, with no siren or lights on, pulled up outside and two police officers got out – in rather too leisurely a fashion, in my opinion. I'd jumped up and opened the front door before they had time to ring the doorbell, trying to usher them upstairs, but they insisted on coming into the lounge, sitting on the other sofa and taking down a few details first in their notebooks.

'We've rung the RSPCA and they're contacting their snake expert,' announced the taller one after I'd finished giving what information I had. 'There may be a bit of a delay owing to this expert being called away to another emergency.'

Bel gasped.

Good God! How many of those creatures are on the loose today? I thought to myself.

'Have you identified it, sir?'

'Sorry?'

'Have you identified it? What kind of snake is it?'

'It's a snake and a bloody big one. That's all I know.'

'Yes sir, but what kind? So the snake man knows what he's dealing with.'

'I've absolutely no idea. Take a look yourself.'

'We just want someone to take it away!' my wife said in an anguished voice.

The police officers exchanged glances, then went upstairs.

'I don't think it would be wise to open that door,' said the shorter one. 'He might be waiting on the other side, ready to strike.'

They contented themselves with peering at the blurred shot that I'd managed to take on my phone, just before I'd slammed the bathroom door.

So we amused ourselves while waiting for the cavalry to arrive by Googling 'snake, black and orange patterned' and a number of possibilities came up. Many of them were described as 'harmless to humans' but Bel didn't seem any calmer and, frankly, neither was I. A snake is a snake, especially if it's five feet long.

* * *

Eventually, a bald man in black uniform and gloves turned up, carrying a hessian sack and a pole with two prongs on the end of it.

'Brian… I do the snakes,' he introduced himself with a wave. 'Where is 'ee then? Bathroom, is it?'

I replied in the affirmative and he nodded as if people found snakes in their bathrooms all the time.

The idea, he cheerfully explained to us, was to carefully pin down the snake with the pole, then bundle it into the sack, tie up the sack and cart it away to safety. Safety? I was more worried about *my* safety, not the snake's.

'Can't you just kill it? It's a danger to the public, surely?'

'Oh no, sir, I couldn't do that. Not unless 'ee's really ill. This is someone's cherished pet. Besides, from the description, 'ee sounds 'armless enough. But I've got to catch 'im first.'

So we all trooped upstairs (except Bel, who by this time had definitely had enough and announced she was going to stay at her sister's house until we'd caught the damn thing) and the snake man carefully opened the door a crack. ''Ee's not round the lav any more,' he announced cheerily. 'I'll just go in for a closer look.'

I shrank back. The police officers stood poised, though what they'd do if a dirty great snake lunged at them, I didn't know and I'm sure they didn't either. The snake expert gingerly entered the bathroom.

''Ee's not in the bath,' he called. 'Nor the shower cubicle. Not behind the door and not in the basin. Let's look inside the lav. They like it in there.'

He lifted up the loo seat and peered inside. Nothing.

'What you have 'ere, sir, is the 'oudini of snakes. 'Ee's escaped.'

'What do you mean, escaped? It must be there somewhere.' I felt myself sweating. 'Try the towel rail. Is it behind it? Could it be hiding somewhere?'

'I've looked everywhere, sir. Towel rail, laundry bin, bathroom bin… and I can assure you, 'ee's not 'ere. I know all their 'idey 'oles, believe you me, and being as it's a snake, they've got a lot of places to 'ide, I'll give you that. But 'ee's not 'ere.'

'Could it have escaped under the door?'

'Unlikely, given the towel you stuffed under it.'

'Where is it then?'

'I think, sir, 'ee's done a runner, so to speak, or rather a *dive*, down the lav.'

'*What?*'

''Ee's slithered down the toilet, is my guess. That'll be 'ow 'ee got in, most prob'ly. 'Ee'll be in yer pipes now. Could end up in a completely different 'ouse. Or not. If you get my drift.'

I couldn't believe what I was hearing.

The taller police officer stepped forward. 'So what you're saying is…'

'Wot I'm saying is, 'ee's gone. For now, anyway. I'll check the rest of yer 'ouse, obviously, but I don't 'old out much 'ope. That's snakes for you. Clever little buggers. Anyway, it sounds like what you 'ave 'ere is a corn snake. You don't want to be worrying about 'im. No danger to the public. No danger at all. Got any pets, have you? Any mice? Rats…?'

I said we hadn't.

'Right, well, if 'ee turns up again, just give me a buzz. 'Ere's me direct number. If I don't answer just leave a voicemail. I've been very busy recently, for some reason. Think it's the 'ot weather.'

With that, the man headed off in the direction of the other rooms, turning round to add, 'Oh, keep the loo seat down. With a 'eavy book on it. Just in case.'

This was not going as planned. I'd thought the snake expert would simply remove the snake and that would be the end of it. For one thing, I couldn't see Bel setting foot in the house again until it had been found. She'd already fled to her sister's. I didn't want to stay here myself, come to that. What if they never found it? It could make itself a home in my house, and one day I'd be on the loo, or in the shower, then suddenly it would appear and…

Good God. What were we going to do? What was Bel going to do? She wouldn't be able to take it, not coming so soon after the other incident.

My wife had been talking about moving house for ages. She wanted to move closer to her mother in Bournemouth. This snake thing could tip her over the edge. Maybe it was time to go on an extended holiday, at least, until the thing had been found. And if it never turned up, well, maybe we *could* sell the house and move to the South Coast. I'm near retirement age as it is. A change of scene might be just what we could do with. No need to tell the buyer about our unusual house guest. No need at all…

* * *

Ted had finished his tale of our friend's unwanted visitor.

'Imagine something like that happening round here! Who'd have thought it? It's amazing what people keep in their houses these days.' He shook his head with wonder. 'I heard they're still looking for it. They put an appeal out on the local news the other day for the owner to come forward.

'According to Ian, Geoff and Bel are definitely thinking about moving out now. She's not been back to the house since. Still staying at her sister's. Word is, they're leaving the area completely. Going to the South Coast.'

'Moving out? Are they now? That's interesting. Anyway, Ted, I'll have to finish this another day if you don't mind.' I laid the shovel carefully on the ground. I'd already dug about a quarter of the pond. 'You see, it's time for my lunchtime shift at Animal House. You know, near the station. The pet shop.'

SHOPPING TRIP

'Excuse me dear, which is the way out? Could you show me, please?'

Evelyn had approached the thirty-something man in skinny black jeans, black polo shirt and black designer trainers on the confident assumption that he would be able to guide her to the exit. Ideally, he'd take her elbow and walk her there himself, personally, like a shop assistant would have done in the old days. Still did, occasionally, in her local Waitrose. Such lovely polite young men they had in there.

'Sorry dear, I don't work here. I'm as lost as you are!'

With that, the man was off, hastily retreating from the smartly dressed, petite woman – in a cornflower blue suit with her bouffant silver hair and black patent heels – before she had a chance to trap him with more conversation. It was bad enough having to trek through this vast cavern of a home store, following a path which took you past so many departments – sofas, beds, pictures, curtains and toys – when all you wanted was a pack of tealights, some cheap paper napkins and maybe a lightbulb.

He felt like he'd been in the shop for hours. He glanced at his mobile. He *had* been in the shop for hours. Where the hell was Patrick, anyway? He couldn't even get a signal on his phone. The man headed off in the rough direction of the exit (he wasn't lost at all; that had just been a ploy to get rid of the woman).

Meanwhile, Evelyn, short of stature but determined, was slowly making her way around the outdoors department. She had been about to redouble her quest to find the exit when her attention was drawn to the houseplants that had been ready planted in smart grey and cream ceramic containers. Such reasonable prices! Much cheaper than her local garden centre. Perhaps she should buy a couple? She loaded two into her trolley, which was already quite full, then propped her walking stick precariously on the top, followed by her smart black leather handbag.

Marvellous, these trolleys. Like a Zimmer frame, really, on wheels. Of course, she wouldn't be seen dead using a Zimmer frame, but the trolleys really were rather handy for getting you around the shop, even if they were a bit on the heavy side. If she got tired and there was nowhere to sit down, she could simply lean on the trolley for a few minutes until she got her breath back.

Never mind the queue of people behind her who were silently cursing this tiny woman in front who was holding them up in the middle of the aisle. Not so silent either, some of them, but her hearing aid was temperamental at the best of times so Evelyn was blissfully unaware of the trouble she was causing.

She carried on walking. Was this where you were supposed to go – oh, look at those table lamps! *I'll just have a quick squizz at them*, she thought to herself. The prices here really were very reasonable indeed. Of course, you had to pick your item carefully. She didn't much care for some of the curtains she'd seen earlier, which looked flimsy and see-through in her opinion. Cheap. Those saucepans now, they would never stand up to repeated use. Still, young people never seemed to cook these days. It was all takeaways and going to Nando's, if her 25-year-old nephew was to be believed.

Now she was threading her way through the sofas. Surely, she'd been here once already today? That one over there – it looked rather comfy. Such a nice floral pattern, but not too chintzy. A bit like June's, only cleaner. Evelyn had told her friend not to get the one with the cream background, but she never listened. That moulting cat didn't help, either. Fancy buying pale upholstery when you had a jet black furball. Madness.

Perhaps she could just have a little sit down on it, try it out… Of course, she wasn't actually looking for a sofa. Her old one did the job perfectly well and, anyway, they'd never get this one through the door at The Firs. They would have to push it through the French windows at the back, and even then it might get stuck. What a to-do *that* would be. After all, remember the fuss last year about Evelyn's niece parking her baby buggy on the landing, just for a couple of hours, while she had tea with her aunt. There'd been not one complaint from the other residents, but Maureen had still got annoyed with her and said it would have to be moved into Evelyn's own flat. They'd only just managed to squeeze it through the front door, then one of the wheels had left mud (at least, she hoped it was mud) on her beige carpet.

When you thought about it, Maureen had been a bit funny right from the start, especially when Evelyn had said she wasn't moving into the retirement flats unless she could have a gardener once a week to tidy the spot outside her ground floor window.

'But Evelyn, we have a gardener who already comes round once a fortnight to keep the whole grounds tidy. We can't have him coming round especially for you. There would be *complaints*.'

'I just like things tidy, Maureen. I can see some weeds from here. Look at that!' She glared through the window at a dandelion.

'Well, if you feel that strongly, Evelyn, you could always have a go at the weeding yourself. It's wonderful exercise, you know. Very therapeutic and it keeps you supple. Lots of our residents like pottering about in the garden. I could lend you a trowel if you like. I can see you're still sprightly!'

'Oh no, dear, I don't do weeding. Not if there's a decent box set I want to watch.'

That had shut the woman up, and Evelyn had got her way, at least partly. The gardener still only came once a fortnight, but he made sure he tidied her patch before doing the rest of the grounds. She was in the flat on sufferance, anyway. Once Ron had died, there seemed no point keeping on the four-bedroomed house at the top of the hill. Her children and grandchildren rarely visited her, so what did she need all that room for? The house was just full of things gathering dust.

When her eldest, Mark, had suggested the Firs, she had resisted at first, but once she had visited at an open day, she had to admit that it did have a lot of advantages.

The old house was getting a bit much, what with all the cleaning and maintenance it needed. She had a cleaner but Evelyn had a suspicion that she didn't get too much cleaning done. Certainly not upstairs, when Evelyn wasn't there to watch over her. She wouldn't put it past her to switch on the Hoover and then sit down and start texting friends, instead of actually using the thing.

The catering here was another plus, of course. There was a restaurant if she didn't fancy cooking, and if you were ill you could get somebody to bring up lunch on a tray. The meals weren't exactly gourmet standard but they were perfectly acceptable, if a bit too much on the 'nursery comfort food' theme. Evelyn used 'room service' quite a bit when she was just fed up of the others' company and wanted to eat in peace and quiet.

They had regular residents' shopping trips, so she hardly needed to use her car, although she liked going for a drive once in a while, like today, just to maintain her independence. They went on organised outings to theatre matinees or concerts. Apparently, a hairdresser visited every week. Evelyn still liked to catch up on the gossip at Snips in the High Street. It was nice to know there was someone on hand to touch up your roots if you needed it in an emergency. She was only a mile from the old house so she could still keep in touch with her old neighbours – which was just as well, given the state of some of the other residents.

That Rosemary on the floor above, who'd been at The Firs six months longer than Evelyn, was all right, and the two of them often had a good gossip about the other 'inmates', as they called them. Only in the privacy of their own flats though, as Evelyn was convinced the communal areas were being bugged by Maureen. She wouldn't have put it past her to kick out one of the 'guests', as Maureen insisted on calling them, if she thought they were causing trouble. Evelyn already had past form on that front. She'd only been there a week when she led a residents' revolt to get proper china cups for their tea rather than the horrible, garish mugs that looked like they'd come from the pound shop.

She yawned. This shopping business was all rather tiring. She'd seen it as a little adventure when she set off in her car this morning, but now it was – gracious! Past four o'clock and she ought to be going home. Back to The Firs, anyway. Still, she'd had a lovely lunch in the restaurant, even if it was self-service. Salmon with new potatoes and vegetables and the price was ever so reasonable. Evelyn paused. She had the distinct sense that she'd forgotten something. What could it be?

She gazed around for a bit, watching the other shoppers, and then remembered with triumph. That was it. Her trolley! Where had she last had it? Beds, was it? She'd better try and find her way back. At least her memory was still working, which she put down to doing the crossword in the newspaper every day. She had started to have one delivered to her room because Dougie, one of the few men at The Firs, was likely to steal the communal paper and tear out the crossword before anyone else could get to it. Even then, he didn't actually complete the thing, as Evelyn had been pleased to notice.

She hobbled off in what she thought was the direction of the bed department. She spotted an unlabelled door – was that a shortcut? Well, it didn't say 'No Entry' or 'Staff Only'. Opening it, Evelyn found she was in a roomset – a sort of bedsit by the look of it, with the bedroom in the same room as the kitchen. Must be intended for students.

When she'd started working in London, her accommodation had been the box room of an old house with four others. Five people using one bathroom, and no shower, just a bath, which took hours to fill. If you weren't first or second in the queue, you didn't even get any hot water until the tank filled up again. Early mornings had been a nightmare so she used to get up at six, well before everyone else, just so she could use the bathroom in peace. Even now, after more years than she cared to remember, she was still an extremely early riser.

In contrast, youngsters these days didn't realise they were living in such luxury. She'd been horrified to find out from her nephew that university students living in hall had their own ensuite bedrooms. Whatever next? Their own personal butler? No wonder they were all in debt by the time they left college.

At least at The Firs, she had a proper, separate kitchen and a sitting room, with a tiny spare bedroom. Her son had wondered how on earth they were going to fit a lifetime of possessions into the new place, but he needn't have worried. When Evelyn set her mind to something, she got it done efficiently and without fuss. The day she moved was the day the local charity shop had a bonanza, considerably increasing their stock of china ornaments, floral blouses and 'timesaving' gadgets.

She had been worried about what she would do when she had visitors, but when she had mentioned this to Mark, he had said, as quick as a flash, 'Don't you worry, Mum, we can easily stay at the hotel up the road. Much easier for you.' In the event, she didn't have all that many visitors, anyway, what with Mark being so busy all the time on his trips for work. Or so he said.

Sandra, his wife, was an ineffectual sort of woman who never came to see her mother-in-law on her own. In truth, she was a little scared of Evelyn, although she'd never admit it. In any case, the grandchildren had all left home now, busy with their own jobs. What visits she got revolved mainly around Christmas and birthdays.

She'd had to spend last Christmas at The Firs as Mark and Sandra had treated themselves to a cruise around the Caribbean. Imagine! Spending his inheritance before he'd even received it. She'd moaned about it before they went, mainly to make them feel guilty, but had actually quite enjoyed festivities at The Firs. A lot of the residents had been carted off by dutiful relatives so there were only a few of them left; but luckily, her friend Rosemary was still there, as was Dougie, who spent a lot of the day complaining about the lack of his usual newspaper.

The staff had taken them to the lovely carol service at the church and then the chef had really come up trumps with the Christmas dinner. By bribing her favourite member of staff, Evelyn had made sure there was enough alcohol on hand to liven up the atmosphere.

By the time the Queen's Speech came on, they were all a little tipsy, some of them even standing to attention for the National Anthem. Dougie even started saluting, which Evelyn thought was going a bit far. She managed to commandeer the TV remote so that she could pick which films to watch, and in the evening those who were still awake had a singsong around the piano, played by ninety-year-old Mr Fletcher (nobody ever called him by his first name, probably because nobody had a clue what it was).

* * *

Back in the store, Evelyn was still exploring the roomset. It was amazing what they could do these days when it came to saving space. It was down to all those students, she supposed, needing somewhere to live. Thousands of them, who saw it as their right to go to university, not a privilege. Not like in her day. She'd never gone. Her parents couldn't afford it, for a start.

Anyway, becoming a personal assistant had been a perfectly respectable job back then. You did that for a few years and then you got married to your boss or another equally suitable man. It had worked for her. But now it was all equal rights and women had to do it all – reach the top of their career, churn out children, look after the home *and* care for elderly relatives. It was no wonder there were all these divorces.

She opened a cupboard door. Now this would be ideal for storing all her tins. It had a clever rotating shelf that you could turn round to get to things at the back. She pushed it experimentally. Then she spotted the shoe storage – she could have done with that… Evelyn had had to throw out a lot of things before she moved into The Firs but she wouldn't be parted with her shoes. Even the ones she used for dancing that she hadn't worn in years. She used to love dancing at the Palais on Saturday nights…

She turned her attention to the bed. Now that really *was* ingenious. There was a diagram next to it which showed how it had a sort of spring so that it could fold up during the day, right up against the wall, if you needed the extra living space. Marvellous what they came up with these days, she thought, as she perched on the edge.

Once she was sitting down, Evelyn realised just how tired she was. She must have walked miles in this store. Back in the flat, it would have been time for her afternoon nap. Not that Evelyn let on to anyone that she slept in the afternoon. To tell the truth, she was a teensy bit ashamed about it. Only old people did that, surely?

She really must think about finding the way out soon. But Evelyn found now she didn't want to move one more step. Tramping round this place had definitely tired her out, especially as she wasn't normally so active. At The Firs, she didn't even have to negotiate stairs if she didn't want to, seeing as how she was on the ground floor. Besides, there was a lift at the flats.

The bed was surprisingly soft and she managed to lift her legs up on to it. *I'll just have a little lie-down*, she thought to herself. *Ten minutes and then I'll feel up to finding the exit.*

* * *

The next morning

As usual, Dale was on his early cleaning shift. He trundled his vacuum cleaner around the store, humming along to the latest download emanating from his earphones (he'd had two warnings from his supervisor but continued to wear them at work). He liked it best at this time, before the hordes arrived. In fact, he only had five more days to go before he was off on holiday to Florida with his girlfriend. The holiday wasn't cheap but he had saved up all the money from his cleaning job, and done overtime as well.

It was probably because his thoughts were on his forthcoming holiday that he failed to see the rather frail looking figure lying flat out on the bed in the new section, still closed to the public, her stick resting next to her, even though he must have passed within just a couple of metres. He couldn't fail to notice, however, an abandoned trolley that was stuffed full of vases, picture frames, lampshades and cushions, with two pot plants (slightly wilting) teetering precariously on top. *Better move that*, he thought, remembering what his supervisor had said just the other day about trip hazards.

* * *

Half an hour later

It was opening time – later than usual since it was a Sunday. Stan, who'd been a security guard at the store for more than five years, never ceased to be amazed by how many people he found queuing up to get in every morning. He unlocked the huge glass doors and customers rushed in purposefully. Some were on a mission to find something in particular, others just came for a day out. Hadn't they got anything better to do on a Sunday? Apparently not. In half an hour or so, long queues would already be forming at the checkouts as people wrestled with flatpack furniture, lampshades and rugs. Just another day for the store.

* * *

Meanwhile, a petite woman in a slightly rumpled jacket, with a rather flattened perm, carrying a stick and a smart handbag, was hobbling up to a man dressed in denim shorts and flip-flops who was examining the picture frames.

'Excuse me, dear, which is the way out?'

DESPERATE MEASURES

'I've got some news,' he said as he came through the front door, flinging his jacket over the bannister. He was later than usual, the telltale smell of alcohol on his breath. For once, Amanda was cooking, stirring something unidentifiable in a large saucepan on the stove, rather than practising her yoga positions or shopping on the Internet. As usual, the nanny had put the children to bed hours ago. All was quiet upstairs.

'You won't like it.'

'You forgot to book those flights, didn't you? I *told* you to book them today before they go. I know it's almost a year ahead but if we leave it later they'll have none left. October half-term is when everyone wants to go to the Caribbean these days.'

'We'll talk about the flights later. It's something else.'

'That week off? Someone else got in first? Because I told you not to—'

'It's not that.'

'Then what? What is it?'

'I've been made redundant.'

There was silence in the kitchen save for the sauce bubbling on the stove.

'What?'

'Laid off.'

'*What?*'

'Stop saying, "What?" You heard me the first time.'

'Is this a joke?'

'Before you ask, I don't know why they picked me. There are newer people who could have gone. People who have only been with the firm for five minutes. They said it was the job. Not needed any more. "Surplus to requirements." Not me personally. The job.'

'Then why couldn't they find you something else? Use you elsewhere in another department? Remember what Hutton said—'

'I know what Mr bloody Hutton said. But that was last year's annual review and everything's changed since then. The market's changed. They probably didn't ask his opinion at all. It didn't come from him. It was Van der Gelt. His boss. I didn't see it coming at all.'

'Well, you'll just have to talk to him. Go back and—'

'No. That's not the way it works. It's done now. I should have seen it coming. When our closest rival started laying people off last year, I knew it was a possibility for us. But not my department. Not sexy but safe as houses – they always say that about us. But not this time. Three of us are going. Half of the entire department.'

'I just can't believe it. Are you sure you can't—'

'I've told you, there's nothing I can do. It's all settled. I had to clear my desk today with a security guard standing over me. It was most embarrassing. Remember what they showed on TV years ago, when that bank collapsed? People walking out of their office with cardboard boxes? Well, there's a cardboard box of my stuff in the hall. I had to come home by taxi. All I've got to show for giving nine years of my life to that place. They took away my security pass so I can't set foot in there again. Can't say a proper goodbye to everyone. Not that I want to.'

'I can't believe it. Tell me it's not a joke. *Are* you joking?'

'I am *not* joking, believe me.'

'What are we going to do? There are the school fees, and you haven't paid the balance on that holiday…'

'Let's not worry just yet. I get three months' redundancy pay. And Mum and Dad will pay the school fees if I ask them nicely. I'll start looking around for something. Contact the agencies. They bothered me enough when I was in work, now they can earn their commission for me. There's always a bit of consultancy work.'

'What about the holiday? I've been looking forward to it ever since Barbados.'

'I don't think we can justify it now. We'll have to cancel.'

'But we've paid the deposit and that was over a grand as it is. We'll have to go. I *must* have a holiday! You don't know what it's like, what with the children…'

'Stop going on about the bloody holiday! Didn't you hear? I'VE LOST MY JOB.'

'I'll have to go back to—'

'No. I won't have you working. Not with the children to look after. None of my colleagues' wives work. It's not right.'

Amanda allowed herself a tiny sigh of relief. Thank goodness. She hadn't really been seriously suggesting that she should go back to work. She couldn't stand that after all these years. Besides, when would she get the time for all her gym workouts, manicures and massages? Jeremy would just have to find another job. That was all there was to it.

Six months later

'Look, Jeremy, it's just not working. How are we expected to live like this? I thought you'd have gone back to paid employment long before now. It's been six months for God's sake. I've had to exist without a personal trainer for *six months!*'

'Calm down, will you? These things take time. I can't just walk into a job. It's a bad time in the market at the moment. Everyone says so. We'll have to think creatively. Maybe I should do something completely different. Nothing to do with banking. I'm always reading about those ex-financiers who come up with an idea for a new food product, trot off to Waitrose and get a huge contract to supply it in their stores. Perhaps I could do something like that.'

'*Jeremy!* I want sensible suggestions!'

'Well, *you* come up with something then. Otherwise, you'll have to go back to work.'

'Right, I will. eBay.'

'What do you mean, eBay? I thought I told you not to go on it again. We can't afford it now.'

'No silly, I don't mean buying stuff on it. *Selling* things. Remember when we sold that horrible mirror your parents gave you?'

'And the buyer turned up and said they were getting on the bus with it? It was so huge, they probably smashed it on a lamppost before they got home.'

'Yes, but we made money, didn't we? Cash. Tax-free.'

'Yes but…'

'Well, look here. I've been selling all this stuff on eBay for the past month. That giftcard your aunt gave us for that downmarket store. I wouldn't set foot in that place if you paid me. What could we possibly want to buy from there? Or there's that vase we got for our wedding from the McAllisters. Remember? It's so terribly ugly! But a lady from Wolverhampton didn't think so. She was delighted with it. Then there was that leather jacket you've never worn.'

'I was saving that jacket for a special occasion! It wasn't yours to give away.'

'I didn't give it away. I sold it. It doesn't fit you now, anyway. You're too fat. It's gone. So I'm putting the children's toys on next. That old bike that Sophia's too big for. And Hamish's scooter. Here's the money I've got so far.'

They were in the kitchen. She opened one of the tall Farrow & Ball painted cupboards that had cost a fortune to be specially designed and lifted out a large tin that had once contained posh hot chocolate.

'Open it.'

Jeremy prised off the lid, took out a sheaf of crumpled notes and counted them.

'There's over five hundred pounds here! Why didn't you put this in the bank? What if we'd been burgled?'

'With interest rates being what they are, it's hardly worth the trouble,' retorted his wife. 'Besides, I didn't want the taxman to know.' And she didn't want Jeremy to know that she'd made more, much more than that, but had already spent it on lunches with friends, organic coffees and trips to the hypnotherapist. And other 'essentials'. Well, she had a lifestyle to maintain. Thank goodness Douglas and Annabel had agreed, albeit reluctantly, to fund the school fees; otherwise, they would have been in real trouble.

A year later

'Jeremy! I'm talking to you! *Did you get the email?*'

'Yes.'

She looked at his face. 'You didn't get it, did you? You didn't get the job. The job you said you would definitely get. Because Jurgen had recommended you. You didn't get it. The dead cert.'

'No. I didn't get it.'

'Why not?'

'How should I know? Bloody internal candidate, probably.'

'Look Jeremy. Look around this house. Have you noticed what's happened? Have you?'

He looked around. 'Apart from the dust caused by the lack of a cleaner, do you mean? Hang on… what's that gap there, on the wall?'

'"That gap" used to be filled by that painting your mother gave us. I never liked it. It's gone. Sold. As is the

Moroccan pouffe you brought back on that business trip. It was never comfortable anyway.

'But it's not enough, Jeremy. We can't live off our savings and keep remortgaging forever. We need more money. And I know how to make it.

'There's one thing we haven't sold which could fetch us plenty of money. Enough to live on for a year or more, while you find another job. If it's not too much trouble.'

'What's that? There's nothing in this house that... Not my sports car, for God's sake. I draw the line at that. It's my one extravagance.'

His eyes travelled the room, alighting on something gently snoring on the Persian rug. 'I know... what about that? He's costing us a fortune in food and vet's bills. That last operation cost nearly a thousand pounds! Can't we get rid of him?'

'*Jeremy!*' Amanda gathered up the large ball of white fluff into her arms and buried her face in it, causing it to emit a strangled meow. Through the fur, she said, 'If Marmaduke goes, I go. How can you be so heartless?'

'OK, OK, it was only a joke. Marmaduke stays. Who would want him anyway? So what could we possibly sell now? The cottage?'

'Are you mad? With house prices the way they are? We'd get back half what we paid for it. And besides, everyone knows we have a little bolthole in Salcombe. How embarrassing if they found out we'd had to sell it. What would I tell the girls?'

'Then what do you suggest we do now? Should I sell one of my kidneys to some bloke in Turkey so that we can make a few quid from it? *Well, should I?*'

By the tone of his voice, even Amanda could tell her husband was close to exploding. This rare occurrence happened, on average, once a year. At this point in their exchange of words, she usually found it prudent to change the subject to safer ground. Even Amanda knew her limits. But not this time. They were in an Emergency Situation and she had found the perfect way out.

'Don't be silly, Jeremy. As I was saying, there's one thing left we can sell.'

'Well?'

'The children.'

'The children's what? I thought you'd sold lots of their things already. We needed a toy clear out anyway. Thank goodness we cancelled the riding lessons. And did you send the tuba back?'

'No. The children. Sell the children. God knows, they're just an almighty drain on us.'

'Sell the children? On some auction site, I suppose? If that's your idea of a joke, it's not funny at all.'

'Not on eBay, silly. What a ridiculous idea! How could we possibly do that? They have rules about that sort of thing. I'm sure it says no livestock. No, I mean sell them to Americans. I've done all the research on the Internet. There are childless couples who'd pay a fortune. Just think of the money we'd save!

'No more birthday presents, no shoes to grow out of, no expensive parties, no school fees, no handouts when

they're at university, no wedding receptions to fund…
I've worked out exactly how much money we'll save
per child, allowing for inflation, of course. I know your
parents are paying the school fees at the moment but
couldn't they just transfer that money directly to us? It's
not as if they'd miss it.

'We could start with Elodie, she's the prettiest, then
I think Sophia… what do you think? Or maybe one of
the boys next… I've already contacted an agency. They
want to meet us next week. They call it "adoption" but
it's basically selling the children. They can do all the
paperwork. They say we are the first people in the UK
to contact them. Imagine that! You'd think it would be
a really popular service. Apparently, it's normally people
from Third World countries who sell their kids. I said
to the agency, we'll be wanting higher fees than those
people, obviously. But they were fine with that and are
really eager to meet us. They said we can get more money
as the children already speak perfect English. So that's
a bonus. And, of course, they're house trained. Well,
mostly.

'I've booked the flights already. The agency is in the
US – did I mention? On your credit card. The kids can
stay with my mother. Give her something to do. God
knows, she spends enough time at her bridge sessions.
So it's all arranged. I rang her last week and told her you
had a job interview out there.'

Jeremy, standing perfectly still, regarded his wife
through haggard eyes. She looked, as much as he could
tell through all the Botox, deadly serious.

'OK darling, you win. It's a wonderful idea. Fantastic. That should solve all our problems. I'm amazed we didn't think of it before. How clever you are! It will save us thousands. Thousands! Before we sort out all the details, I just need to make a quick phone call. In my study. Just a quick call to an agency about a job. Back very soon.'

He edged out of the room and retreated to the one space in the house that could still make him feel relatively calm, closing the door behind him. His sanctuary. Sitting at his smoked glass desk on a genuine Eames chair that his wife, miraculously, hadn't yet sold, he let out a long breath, then dialled a familiar number. While he waited, Jeremy gazed through the open shutters at the other husbands and wives briskly walking past, returning from the jobs they still had, hurrying to be out of the cold and with their children.

At the other end, someone answered. At last. 'Hallo? Is Dr Grace there? I'm so sorry it's late. He is? Oh, thank goodness. It's Jeremy Bridges here. Could you please tell him it's about my wife. Yes, again. The medication he prescribed last time doesn't seem to be working any more. I think we need a stronger dose. In fact, I think this time we have a real emergency on our hands…'

FULL UP

Everyone in the village knew Adrian Fawcett's house, even if they didn't know his name and had never seen the occupant. It wasn't a difficult house to spot, once you knew what you were looking for. Crockingford was a pretty, prosperous sort of place, the kind of village that estate agents called 'leafy' and was populated by what the marketing people referred to as 'ABC1' types.

It had a main street, consisting of a corner shop, a newsagent, a rather shabby looking café and a 'fireworks emporium'. No one knew why the fireworks shop was there – outside of November and New Year, it never seemed to do any business – but it had existed for years. On the village green, next to the cricket club's hut, there was also a highly regarded pub, the Laughing Parrot, to which people would drive from miles around for Sunday lunches, and where, it was said, a group of Ramblers had once been unceremoniously turned away for wearing boots that were too muddy. There was a thriving primary school which still featured small class sizes, and a luxury car showroom just outside the village boundary full of expensive convertibles, but that was about it, apart from the private houses, of course.

Off the main street were several lanes, and it was down Peartree Lane, the last of these (or first, if you were coming into the village from the opposite direction) that Adrian's house could be found. Down here, each dwelling was individual, detached and boasting quite a substantial garden. Well, they had been large gardens until everyone started building on them. Over the years, all the original brick houses had been knocked down and replaced with something twice or even three times the size: 'Surrey mansions', complete with mock pillars, carports, surveillance cameras, high hedges, topiary, electric gates, tennis courts and even staff quarters – all the trappings that allowed the residents to show off their wealth.

Except for one house, the last one in the lane, which was set back from the road and boasted neither electric gates nor a fancy garage with au pair accommodation on top. This house was the original one, indeed the only one left, dating from the fifties. All the other houses had names – Orchard House, Woodlands, that kind of thing – but this one just had its original number on an ancient gatepost that just about managed to stay upright. Number 24. Leylandii, planted years ago, had grown ridiculously high and seemed to dwarf the modest little house, plunging it into shadow for most of the day. If you really wanted to, though, you could walk up the weed-peppered gravel and peer between the gaps in the hedge. Instead of the manicured lawns and immaculate, sweeping gravel drives that were found outside all the other houses, there was something quite different about number 24.

It was the rubbish. Mounds of rusting car parts, black binbags overflowing with planks of wood, old tin cans (their contents now anonymous since the labels had been bleached by the sun), and teetering piles of paving stones and plastic plant pots, many of them cracked... If a rare ray of sunshine managed to penetrate through the trees, a black and white cat could sometimes be spotted perching on one of the piles, sunning itself while lazily regarding its territory, its paw occasionally swishing at passing flies, its tail twitching languidly.

Had you ventured any further over the threshold (and hardly anyone did, save for the postman, the milkman and the paperboy) and it happened to be first thing in the morning, you would have seen their goods piled up outside the front door. The postman had long since given up trying to push letters through the flap, since it seemed to be jammed tightly shut. Instead, he placed any deliveries in an old cardboard box which was left on the doorstep. The paper boy just dumped the papers on the ground for the same reason, next to the glass bottles left by the milkman.

Had you rung the front doorbell, you would not have got a reply. The windows yielded no clues as the blinds were always down and there was a general unkempt air about the place, as if no one had lived there for years. Yet someone was emptying the cardboard box daily. The milk bottles (one semi-skimmed every two days) and daily papers (three broadsheets and two tabloids a day, extra at weekends) were always removed promptly. Someone was definitely living there.

You might have had more luck if you'd knocked on the side door. Then again, you might not. Mrs Dobby knocked one day. A rather robust individual, she lived a few doors down at number 16 (or Yew Tree Cottage, as she preferred to call it) and one day, on her daily walks with Primrose, her apricot coloured miniature poodle, she had become concerned about the occupant of number 24. 'Concerned' was how she put it. 'Nosy' was the word that some of her neighbours might have used. Every street has a Mrs Dobby, who likes to know the comings and goings of everyone else. She was a one-woman Neighbourhood Watch but kind-hearted too, and if she spotted a neighbour in need she would move in, all guns blazing as it were, with offers of help that were difficult to refuse.

Anyway, there was no answer when Mrs Dobby knocked on the front door, and when she tried to call through the letter flap she found it jammed shut, just like the postman and the paperboy had. So she used her initiative and went around the side, stepping around the teetering piles of bricks and a partly dismantled bicycle in search of the back door. She found the side door and rapped several times on the frosted glass, bellowing 'Hello?' for good measure. She was just about to go home and start sorting out the tennis club rota when there was a glimmer of movement from inside the house. Suddenly, there were sounds of a key turning in the lock, then two – no, three – bolts being pulled back. Eventually, the door creaked open to reveal an unshaven man of indeterminate age (*sixties?* thought Mrs Dobby. She prided herself on her powers of observation but, in this case, it was rather hard to tell).

'Yes?' was all the man said. Behind the thick, ancient NHS spectacle lenses (surely, no one else was wearing that style anymore?), his face had the pallor of someone who rarely saw daylight. He was wearing a stained maroon jumper and threadbare chocolate brown corduroy trousers which had definitely seen better days, dark brown sandals, despite the time of year, and was clutching a week-old newspaper to his chest (Mrs Dobby could be sharp-eyed when she wanted to).

'I just wanted to introduce myself,' announced Mrs Dobby, a shade louder than most people would have attempted. 'Florence Dobby. One of the neighbours. I've not met you before. Is there anything you need? Only I was just passing and I thought I'd pop by.' This required a stretch of the imagination, seeing as number 24 was the last house in the row and there was nowhere else she could be trying to get to.

'Ah, err, Adrian Fawcett. No, thank you,' replied the man slowly, his voice slightly croaky, as if it was the first time he'd put it to use for a while. 'I'm perfectly all right. Managing fine. Thank you.' This last phrase was uttered with a certain finality. He started to close the door but Mrs Dobby's gimlet eyes had managed to rove around the interior during their brief exchange.

It was difficult to tell in the gloom but the room had presumably once been a kitchen. It could be called that no longer. In the Belfast sink was a mound of empty baked bean tins. There must have been at least twenty, judging by how tall the pile was. On every other available surface was a stack of newspapers reaching almost to the ceiling. The effect was to create a sort of cave, with a narrow space just wide enough for one person, if they were determined, to pass down the middle. Mrs Dobby noted there were even newspapers on the cooker and shuddered. Was the rest of the place like this?

She'd seen the TV programmes, which basically turned hoarding into entertainment, while claiming that the people involved were being helped to get over their mental health issues. But surely none of the participants had been as extreme as this man. Although there was one instance she remembered when the subject of the programme had to dive in head first just to get into his kitchen, through a tiny gap hardly big enough to fit a person. He had needed help and so did this Mr Fawcett, by the looks of it. Even Mrs Dobby, determined though she was, realised that she was not the right person for the job.

Suddenly she felt something brush her leg and looked down just in time to see a black and white cat shooting out of the door.

'Lovely to meet you,' she called. 'By the way, have you lived here long?'

'Twenty-two years,' was the almost inaudible reply before the door was gently but firmly shut, locked and bolted again.

* * *

A week later

'That man needs help,' said Mrs Dobby at the annual Crockingford Society committee meeting, held in the back room of the Laughing Parrot. There was an unusually large turn-out this year, perhaps helped by the fact that rumours had gone round in advance of the meeting that something was going to be decided about number 24. It seemed that Mrs Dobby was not the only one in the village who was harbouring concerns.

'He can't go on living like that,' she continued to the assembled group of neighbours. 'What if he got seriously ill and nobody noticed? He could die in there and no one would even be able to get to him. I'm sure I saw papers on the hob. What if there's a fire?'

'Serve him right if he does kick the bucket,' muttered a male voice from the back of the room. Heads turned but it wasn't quite clear who had voiced this rather unkind sentiment, although several people had reached the same conclusion as the owner of the voice.

'Never mind that,' said Everard, the accountant from number 20. 'What's he doing to our house prices? That's what I want to know. *And* there are the rats. He should be evicted. I've been saying it for years, if anyone had cared to listen.'

'Hear, hear,' said someone else from the back.

'He needs professional help,' said someone else. 'Why don't we ring Social Services?'

'Why don't we just leave him in peace?' said Josie from number 12, a yoga teacher whose liberal views were, it had to be said, somewhat at odds with most of her neighbours. 'He's not harming anyone.'

'You heard what Mrs Dobby said. That house is a tinderbox just waiting to go up. Newspapers on the stove, for goodness' sake! A group of us should go round and start clearing the grounds. We could take everything to the dump in Alec's van. No good waiting for the professionals. It could take months. You know how slow the council is at getting anything done. I don't trust those social workers anyway.'

'I'll volunteer to help.'

'And me.' And so the meeting rumbled on, amid much disagreement about what was to be done, if anything, about number 24.

As things turned out, though, the work party eventually recruited to remove the vast piles of rubbish from Adrian's property (six men and two women) was not needed. Ten days after the meeting in the Laughing Parrot, sirens were heard in Peartree Lane at two in the morning. Loud noise at that time of night was unheard of (apart from Josie's annual New Year's Eve party, which was tolerated on account of it only being once a year). As worried residents tweaked back their curtains, they saw three fire engines racing towards number 24, Adrian's house, which was easily visible against the night sky by the orange flames that were licking out of the windows, with many of the surrounding trees having been burnt to a crisp already.

It took six hours to bring the blaze under control, with fire crews having to be called from the next county owing to another emergency the same night a few miles away. The next day firefighters would still be there, hosing down piles of combustible material lest they should start another fire. Given the owner of the house, combustible material was not in short supply.

Adrian himself, wearing a chocolate brown, moth-eaten dressing gown, had miraculously been rescued from the house and led away in great distress, being heard to cry, 'My papers! I must save my papers!' It was all the ambulance crew could do to prevent him from wrenching open the back door of their vehicle in order to get back inside his property.

After staying in hospital for a couple of days as a precaution, he was discharged. A few days later, someone found his cat, which must have escaped the house before the flames really took hold, wandering in another garden. Apart from a slight cough and a singed paw, it was fine.

Of course, the fire was the talk of Crockingford, and there was much speculation about its cause. Was it the newspapers on the cooker that Mrs Dobby had recalled seeing? Or was it – as one or two thought privately, but didn't say out loud – the work of Everard from number 20, who had been so desperate to get rid of his neighbour? There was a police investigation but nobody ever did find out, and if anyone did know what had really happened, they certainly weren't telling.

* * *

A week later

Number 24 was still standing but most of the roof and one of its walls had quite literally caved in. If you got as close as you were allowed, right up to the 'No entry' tape put up by the fire crew (as the house had turned into a sort of local tourist attraction), you could see the remains of Adrian's possessions, in sad, charred piles. There was still a smell of charcoal about the place. The newspapers, of course, had been the first to go, fuelling the flames and turning the blaze into an inferno. It was quite hard to identify most of the stuff, although you could see an old-fashioned 'box' television with its insides blown out, and lots of electrical wiring strewn about. Here and there were small pieces of blackened material that had once been curtains, perhaps, and a couple of wooden legs was all that remained of a kitchen chair. The avocado bathroom suite on the first floor was more or less intact, but standing forlornly, open to the elements now that the roof was off and a side wall had disintegrated.

A few people in the village were genuinely concerned about Adrian, including Mrs Dobby, who had gone so far as to visit him in hospital. She had turned up at his bedside armed with flowers and grapes (Adrian pretended to be asleep for her entire visit, though he did appreciate that day's newspaper which she'd also brought with her). But what everyone in Crockingford wanted to know, of course, was what would happen to the house now? Surely, this was an ideal opportunity for someone to take the site off Adrian's hands, demolish the ruined structure and build something more fitting, more in keeping with the neighbouring houses, ready for a nice young family to move in, perhaps?

* * *

Six months later

Adrian

'Well, Jim, I'm not dead, as you can see, despite the rumours put about by some of my neighbours. Wishful thinking, I'm sure. I am perfectly aware that they wanted to see the back of me. Wanted to get me out of that house into a bed and breakfast, or a hostel, or sheltered housing… well, anywhere really, just as long as it was safely away from the village. So that a nice professional, middle class, *tidy* family could move in and replace my old house, which has been my *home* for twenty-two years, with an ugly newbuild. Mow the lawn, pull up the wildflowers, cut down the trees (what's left of them), make it all tidy and boring and *respectable*…' This last word was said with a sneer.

'Well, as it happens, Jim, I *am* leaving the area. You're the first to know. You can put that in your newspaper as an exclusive! I don't talk to the neighbours, funnily enough, so they might as well read it in *The Argus*. I've had enough of being in this temporary accommodation. I'm going to stay with my sister in Eastbourne. Oh yes, I have a sister. Thought I had no family left, didn't you? So did everyone else, I expect. She's ten years older than me, but she's still my sister. She says that now I've changed my ways, I'm welcome to live at her house. It's by the sea so I shall enjoy my daily walks. Might even do them in daylight now!'

He guffawed with laughter at the thought of his newfound freedom. 'And she's even agreed to keep

Pushkin, as long as I give him a flea treatment first. She says at the first sign of any clutter, she'll tip it all in the bin and do you know what, I believe her. Our Phyllis can be very strict at times. She can't bear it if people don't play by the rules. And I didn't play by the rules, did I? I didn't do what society expects you to do. That's why we never spoke for four years, my sister and I, and she hadn't visited me for five – she couldn't bear the thought of entering my house any more.

'She's large, is our Phyllis, and last time she came, she was tripping over my precious things. I couldn't have her upsetting my piles of paper and breaking the vinyl records that I'd collected for years. So I didn't want her around either. I thought I was doing OK, you know? I've always liked my own company. Bit of clutter here and there… well, who hasn't?

'Only it got out of hand, didn't it? I just didn't want to admit it. Phyllis told me it wasn't right, the last time she came round. Said I should get help. I ignored her, of course. Went back to my papers and books. Well, she *was* right. I see that now. Losing everything in the fire… you know what, Jim? It's liberating, that's what it is. If you'd told me that six months ago, I'd never have believed it. Never. But now I'm going to turn over a new leaf, as they say, and get my life back. A new beginning, away from here.

'As for *those people*' – he gestured to the other houses, with their manicured lawns, 4x4s and identikit Farrow and Ball front doors – 'well, I'm having the last laugh. I've sold up but it's not to a family. Oh no. I was approached by a developer who offered me double what anyone else would. He's going to demolish the old house – what's left of it – and build a block of flats. Says he can probably fit at least twelve on my land. He'll make a fortune but he's paid enough for me to live on for the rest of my days. I don't have expensive tastes.

'I know what you're thinking: "The council will never allow it." Well, I did too, until I made a few enquiries. I may *look* decrepit to you, Jim, but I still have a fully functioning brain. I used to be a university lecturer, you know. A *real* university, not one of these jumped up polytechnics. Just because I've lost all my possessions, I can still use a phone and surf the internet at the library, you know.

'Everyone wants to move into villages like this, near the Surrey greenbelt, as long as there's a handy train station and a nice little primary school for the kiddies. Then, once they're living here themselves, if anyone tries to build on the green bits, they go potty. Nimbys – isn't that what the papers call them? Where do they think the building plots are going to come from? Thin air? It's not just wealthy commuters either. From what I've found out, it seems that this council is desperate for affordable housing around here, and they've just introduced a new policy. As long as half the flats on my plot meet that criteria, they'll agree to the scheme. The first my neighbours will know about it is when they get letters through their door from the planners. Of course, they'll appeal – they're good at complaining, I know that only too well – but it won't make any difference if the council has quotas to fill decreed by central government and budgets to stick to. As we all know, developers have deep pockets if they sniff out the possibility of big profits in the future.

'I don't think the building works will go down too well with the sort of people who live round here already, do you? All that chaos and noise while the flats go up. Then, people on benefits moving in, living next to company directors? Cars parked on the verges? Late-night parties? Serves them right,' he chuckled.

'Can you send me a copy of the newspaper article, Jim, when it comes out? I'll give you my sister's address. Much obliged.'

CHANGE OF SCENE

Cassie was annoyed. In fact, she was downright furious. Who had been the one to convince her to book this break in the West Country? Who had said it would be a great idea, a way to de-stress after all that had happened over the past few months – years even; how she could put everything behind her? And who had even offered to pay for it all?

Ed. And where was he now? Back at home, that's where. Assuming he *was* at home and not out with the mysterious Lila. Leaving her and Izzie, who had reached the rebellious teenager stage, on their own as usual. What was so relaxing about that exactly?

'Come *on,* Izz! We haven't got all day.'

Her daughter, dressed in Jack Wills T-shirt, Hollister sweatpants and Converse lace-ups, slopped down the stairs, texting furiously on her iPhone at the same time. 'Mum, we're supposed to be on holiday. Chill out, huh?'

'Look at the time! All the parking spaces will have gone already.'

'Just chill, Mum, OK? It's Cornwall, not London,' said her daughter as she went outside their holiday cottage and clambered into the bright yellow Mini that was accompanying them on this two-week long trip.

From their base in Carbis Bay, near Cornwall's far western tip, it took them just a few minutes to reach the outskirts of the pretty fishing village and artists' colony of St Ives. These days, it was far busier than when Cassie had first visited as a student in her early twenties, staying in a B&B and armed only with a small rucksack and a sketchpad.

She had fallen in love with the place, with everything about it – the scenery, the marvellous light and the quirky characters who made (or at least tried to make) their living from art. She loved going down to one of the beaches or finding a spot on the headland where she could sketch or paint. The contrast with her busy London life, full of parties, friends coming and going was refreshing. She ended up staying for several months after she'd left art college, trying to make a living as an artist herself and hooking up with a surfer who'd come back after travelling the world to live in his hometown.

But then it came to an end. She ran out of money and had to return to London, kissing goodbye to the surfer and saying that she'd return. She never did. She ended up staying at her father's house in Chiswick while she took a succession of low-paid jobs. Bookshop assistant, artist's model, dog walker… Then one day, on a walk by the river, she had met Johnny, who was unlike anyone she'd encountered before. 'A free spirit' her grandmother would have called him, with his shoulder-length black hair tied into a ponytail, his flowery shirts, his houseboat on the Thames near Richmond and his little tan terrier, Bo, constantly by his side.

After two weeks, she'd moved into the houseboat, and ten months later Izzie was born, with blonde hair like her mother, but the rest of her strong features were inherited from her father.

For a time – quite a long time, actually – the three of them were deliriously happy, but free spirits don't like to be tied down forever. While Izzie was still at primary school, Cassie had to reluctantly concede defeat. It was really a wonder that she'd managed to hang on to Johnny for so long.

He sold the houseboat and drifted southwest, ending up in Glastonbury. Cassie and Izzie returned to lodge with Cassie's father but she never completely lost touch with Johnny, who would pop up from time to time, always without warning. He'd shower Izzie with expensive, useless gifts and take her off to a ridiculously posh restaurant that might have been all right if she had been twice the age and not just a child, then disappear again for months. But at least he kept in touch over the years.

They last saw him when he appeared out of the blue on Izzie's sixteenth birthday, bearing a huge bouquet of white roses bearing the logo of a Mayfair florist, whose arrangements were out of the price range of anyone she knew.

'I wanted to be the first man in your life to shower you with flowers, my darling girl!' Johnny boomed, kissing Izzie on both cheeks. Loving the attention, his daughter was in raptures. Cassie was of the opinion that there were more useful things to spend such a large sum of money on – like a decent winter coat, for instance. But that was Johnny through and through. Half an hour later, he was gone –

and neither of them realised that they would never see him again.

His death at the age of 38, from a drugs overdose (accidental or deliberate, they never found out), tragic though it was, was not a complete shock to Cassie. She had always known that Johnny was leading a charmed life. How could he not be, with his rickety motorbike and drinking binges, not to mention his dabbling in an assortment of drugs?

Cassie and Izzie received not a penny when he died, even though Izzie was indisputably his child. Cassie heard that he had at least two other children to support, but the real reason they got nothing, she guessed, was simply because there was no money left. The flowers and everything else had been bought with funds he didn't actually have.

Although they hadn't lived together for years, Cassie still grieved Johnny's death. At the funeral (a humanist service with a cardboard coffin and lots of mourners – mainly female – she'd never met before) her mind was full of *what ifs?* What if she'd carried on living with Johnny? Would they still be living on that houseboat? Would she have been better off? No, worse, probably.

Cassie and Izzie stayed in London, Cassie making a small living and Izzie going to the local state school which, in this part of West London, was full of posh kids.

Then, just as Cassie was thinking that men were too much trouble in the long run, and perhaps she and Izzie were better off on their own anyway, she'd met Ed. She had gone into an antique dealer's near Hampton Court (junk shop was a more accurate description) to have some paintings that she'd inherited from her mother valued. She thought she might have to sell them if her latest job interview didn't turn up trumps. The shop looked deserted so she was about to go outside again when she was suddenly startled by a tall, nattily dressed man in his thirties who stepped out from behind a crammed bookshelf in a dusty corner. He never bought the paintings – he said they were worthless, a claim which Cassie never knew was true or not – but he did get her phone number.

His name was Ed and they soon became a couple – at least, Cassie assumed they were a couple. She always remained a little suspicious of Ed's pretty 'assistant', Lila, however. Half his age and disgustingly slim, she always seemed to be hovering in the background, driving his ancient van when they went off to house clearances, or accompanying him to auctions or early morning sales.

But Cassie liked being with Ed, even if he was somewhat unreliable. She seemed to have made a career of attracting unreliable men. Izzie liked him too, although understandably enough, she didn't have the bond she'd had with Johnny. Cassie hardly saw her daughter these days, anyway; what with Izzie being constantly out with her own friends, and Cassie working all hours at the café. She had no intention of moving in with Ed – that was a trap she didn't want to fall into again.

But as Izzie's school summer holidays approached, it had been Ed who'd suggested a holiday for the three of them. The anniversary of Johnny's death was looming and Cassie was keen to get away from the old haunts in London she had enjoyed with her former lover. Too many memories.

She had already told Ed about her former life in Cornwall, and he was keen to visit the county, which he hadn't set foot in since he was a boy, when he went on family bucket and spade holidays.

'Might look into the local art scene,' he mused when they were in the pub one day. 'It's not the same, of course, now that Wallis and Lanyon and Hepworth are dead. Still, might be able to pick up a little something for the shop. My friend owns a holiday cottage down there. A booking's fallen through and he says that we can stay in it for free for the next two weeks. What do you say to a trip? We can take Mabel.'

Mabel was Ed's ageing but still speedy bright yellow Mini convertible. When the van was off the road he sometimes transported shop items in it. Cassie had seen standard lamps, rolled up Turkish kelims and even an old-school radiator poking dangerously out of the top on those days when he'd got a little carried away with his bargains.

So the holiday was fixed up and Cassie found that she had something to look forward to at last. It would be good to have some time with Izzie after her exams, perhaps for the last time before her daughter went off with her friends on more exotic holidays. She'd bribed her to come by promising a fortnight's sunbathing. (She didn't let on about the unpredictability of the Cornish weather.) Ed would be an interesting travel companion, as long as she made sure he didn't spend too long poking around seaside junk shops. Things were looking better than they had in a long time.

Then disaster struck. A fortnight before they were due to set off, Ed drove Mabel a little too enthusiastically and gained three points on his licence for speeding in Bushy Park. Unfortunately, he already had nine points so it was now illegal for him to drive. 'I wasn't even doing 35mph and the road was deserted!' he protested to Cassie. 'Yes, but the limit's only 20!' she retorted. 'How are we going to get to Cornwall now? You know I can't afford to hire a car, and the train's too expensive.'

'You've got a licence, haven't you? Then you can drive Mabel. I trust you to take care of my pride and joy. Anyway, I was meaning to tell you. I've got some business here that's just come up. Too profitable to turn down. You and Izzie go to Cornwall. You'll have a whale of a time. It might be your last holiday with Izz before she's off clubbing in Ibiza with her friends. Tell you what, here's some cash. I know you're a bit short at the moment. For emergencies only, mind, such as if Mabel gets a puncture. Not for cream teas!' And he winked.

* * *

So here she was, on holiday with Izzie, just the two of them. And actually, it was OK, although she was still fuming at Ed for backing out at the last moment. Was he with Lila, right now…? It was almost as if the speeding ticket had given him a handy excuse not to come. He'd felt so guilty, he'd even given her a wad of cash. Where had that come from? Business must be better than she'd thought. She shook her head. She didn't want to think about all that right now. She wanted to enjoy the brilliant sunshine and the warmth on her face, the huge clotted cream teas and the fresh mackerel, the deep blue sea lapping over the rocks, even the seagulls wheeling noisily overhead, ready to swoop down and steal, in a flash, a whole portion of chips.

Today, they had intended to go to St Ives for a look around. But it was the height of summer and the packed little artists' colony didn't have one inch of room to park. Cassie cursed under her breath. Why hadn't they caught the little train from Carbis Bay? It would have taken five minutes and no need to search for somewhere to park. They'd attempted to drive up the back streets in search of a neglected space, but ended up sitting in a queue of traffic for ten minutes while a 4x4, probably down from the Home Counties, tried to reverse into a tight spot without grazing any other cars or backing into one of the fisherman's cottages, none of which, of course, had front gardens to save them from modern motorised giants.

In the end, there was nothing for it but to head for the big carpark at the top of the hill and then walk down the steep path to town, Cassie sweating and Izzie complaining all the way like a typical teenager.

Then, when they did get down to the harbour, they had to push past hordes of holidaymakers who were more intent on licking every last drop from their melting ice creams than watching where they were going. Lunch was fish and chips sitting on the harbour wall – not that they ate much as they were too busy guarding their fare from the (really rather menacing) seagulls. Izzie said she wanted to go on a boat trip but they were all booked up – rather a relief to Cassie, who felt a little queasy just watching the small boats bobbing out to sea, transferring punters into the slightly bigger (but still too small for her liking) fishing boats for a trip out to Seal Island. They did have a look around the lifeboat station but an interesting tour was spoilt, in her opinion, by the girl at the entrance doing a hard sell, asking for donations when they'd barely got over the threshold.

Lovely though St Ives undoubtedly was, this was not Cassie's idea of a relaxing day out. It was not Cornwall as she remembered it, either. Her happy mood was evaporating. Of course, it was their own fault for coming down in high summer, the busiest time of year, but Cassie wasn't going to pull Izz out of school any earlier and risk the wrath of the head teacher again. She'd already had enough battles over the years involving non-regulation skirts, piercings where they shouldn't be and days off during term time.

Where was Ed when she needed him? She'd tried to call him several times already but his mobile just went to voicemail. There was a nagging thought in the back of her mind that he was enjoying Lila's company, and not just during the day…

Over supper that night in their holiday cottage, Cassie formulated in her mind a change of plan for the following day. The next morning, Cassie ate breakfast on her own, and as soon as Izzie appeared sleepily downstairs, she said, 'Right, change of plan. Get in the car.'

'Where are we going?'

'To buy art. Real art. Not that tourist tat in St Ives.'

'But you haven't any money, Mum. Not enough for pictures, anyway. Why don't we just go to the Tate, buy a few postcards or a book? They've extended it and there's meant to be a great exhibition on there at the moment…'

'We'll do the Tate another day. I do have money. Ed gave me some. It's meant for emergencies but what the hell. He can pay for it. He said he'd pay for the holiday, after all. He owes me something for not being here. Not that I don't love your company, Izz,' she added hastily.

'But I was going to sunbathe today. It's going to be really hot.'

'Plenty of time for that later. We have two whole weeks, remember?' She crossed her fingers, praying the good weather would last. 'We've only just got here. It'll be good for your art studies. Give you inspiration. And you can tan with the roof down.'

Sighing, Izzie clambered into the car. She loved her mother to bits but sometimes the two of them had completely opposing views. She'd wondered if things would have been different with her father around, but he'd left when she was so young, and although he'd visited her from time to time since then, she couldn't really imagine what life would be like with him full-time now. He was dead, in any case, so what was the point in wondering? Anyway, loads of her friends hardly saw their own father.

When Ed had come on the scene, Izzie reflected, her mother had been really happy for a few weeks, but then she'd started having doubts about him. When he was around, he was great but he wasn't exactly reliable, as his failure to materialise for this trip proved. At least he had leant Mum Mabel, so they could be independent. Otherwise, they would have had to cancel the holiday. And at least she was getting a proper holiday this year, even if she couldn't compete with her friends, who all seemed to be going to villas in Majorca or exploring China or something.

Soon, they were whizzing down the twisty lanes, occasionally getting glimpses of the teal-blue sea, peppered with white flecks where it crashed against rocks, the water reflecting a gloriously blue, cloudless sky above. They met a few cars and the occasional tractor, even an incongruous red double-decker bus on a sightseeing trip, but it seemed that most people had headed straight for the beach on such a gorgeous day to enjoy the sunshine.

The day before, Cassie had picked up a leaflet entitled, *Galleries in Penwith*. It mentioned several on the way to Land's End, and trying to get around as many of them as possible felt like a fun way to spend the day. Lying on the beach could wait.

* * *

'What do you think, Izz? For the hallway?'

Izzie regarded the huge oil painting with a wary eye. 'It's very… yellow.'

'Yes, but do you like it?'

'Well… I think so. It's quite big. Are you sure we have room?'

'In the flat? Oh, I'll just have to move things around,' her mother replied airily.

'No, I meant in Mabel.'

'Oh yes, with the roof down I'm sure it'll fit in somehow.'

They managed to fit the painting – a rather large, arresting abstract featuring daubs of yellow paint with a few white and black splodges – into the car's back seat, having to shift the other purchases that Cassie had bought that day in the process. There was a tall ceramic lamp, its shade festooned with seashells, and two hand-embroidered cushions featuring felt fish in luminous colours. A couple of small framed sketches of the Cornish coastline were stored in the boot, along with a large turquoise raku pot that Cassie had thought would look wonderful in their tiny patio garden.

She was having a whale of a time. Buying art and crafts had always been a passion, when she could afford it, and what with the money she'd saved for the trip, plus Ed's cash, she could just about afford to buy several pieces.

She consulted the leaflet. There was one last gallery on her list, in Sennen Cove – the village near Land's End, known principally for its superb surfing opportunities. It was late afternoon now but if they hurried it might still be open. They set off in Mabel and were soon driving down the steep hill into the village. En route to the carpark, they spotted the gallery, sandwiched between a surf shop and a café, and Cassie just had time to glimpse an interesting painting hanging in the window as they drove past. The carpark turned out to be full so Cassie drove out again and started looking for somewhere else to park.

'Did you see that painting, Izz? In the window. Mousehole, it looked like. I must have a closer look. I might buy it.'

'I don't think you're meant to park here, Mum. No one else has except fishermen.'

'Stop fussing. There's nowhere else that I can see.'

'But…'

'It'll be fine. Anyway, I don't think they have traffic wardens down here. Come on.'

Cassie had found a spot by the harbour where there was a space. The only other vehicles there seemed to be ancient vans and small, rusting trucks carrying empty lobster pots, floats and fishing nets. They left the car and headed down steps in the direction of the gallery. Much to Cassie's relief, it was still open. They went inside and she had a good look around the rest of the stock. There were some high-quality pieces and she was just deliberating between the painting she'd seen in the window, and a print of the Jubilee Pool in Penzance that the owner had brought out for her, when she heard Izzie, who had gone outside to sit on a bench in the sun, let out a loud cry.

'*Mabel!*'

Cassie ran to the window. What was the problem? Mabel was parked where she'd left her. Wait a minute… She did a double take. It couldn't be. In slow motion, the little car seemed to be moving backwards, towards the edge of the paved area. As she was registering the fact that there was no wall between the car and the sea, Mabel seemed to gain momentum, and suddenly the little car's wheels reached the edge, then kept going, and before she knew it, the car had kind of belly flopped into the sea, which, it being high tide, was quite deep… It would have been funny if it had been someone else's car, or if it had been in a movie.

Cassie dashed outside. This couldn't be happening. She heard shouts and suddenly wet-suited teenagers were appearing at a run from the nearby surf school, and the man from the ice cream van came out to try and help, but it was too late. Mabel was rapidly being submerged by the waves. Some of Cassie's lovingly collected purchases, including the giant yellow painting, could be seen drifting on the surface of the sea, floating off in the direction of the horizon. The only one which wouldn't be ruined by seawater was the little silver starfish pendant she had bought in Penzance two days before that was now hanging around her neck.

Everything had happened so quickly. Cassie was standing in the middle of the road, gazing out at the scene. Mabel was now fully submerged in the water. You could just make out the car's shape, a yellow mass under the waves lapping against the harbour wall.

Cassie found Izz, who'd run to the water's edge. They looked at each other with horror.

'What are we going to do?' wailed Cassie. 'Ed will kill me!'

'I told you not to park there, Mum! I'm sure Ed said last week that the handbrake was dodgy. Why don't you ever listen to me?' Izz was shouting now, watched with varying degrees of interest and concern by a few passing daytrippers.

'I *do* listen to you! But I…'

She trailed off. Her handbag had suddenly started chirping insistently. Her phone. At least she hadn't left it in the car. She rummaged in her bag and pulled out her mobile.

'Oh no! It's Ed. Of all the times to ring. What can he want? Shall I ignore it?' She put the phone back in her bag. The chirping stopped for a couple of seconds, then started again. Cassie looked at her daughter.

'You might as well answer it, Mum. Get it over with.'

She pressed a button.

'Ed. Listen—'

'No, you listen to me.' His words were breaking up but she could just about make them out. 'Change of plan. I'm coming down now. In fact, we've just passed Plymouth. I'm on the train. No point in driving the van down when you've got the old jalopy. Is she running all right? I've missed her these past few days. The best car I've ever had, that one. I might even treat you two to a cream tea after you've driven me around the sights of the far West. See you at Penzance Station in two hours!'

Cassie switched off her mobile and regarded her daughter, an expression of terror on her face. 'He's on his way down. On the train. Wants us to pick him up in Mabel. Will you tell him or shall I…?'

DOROTHY DAUNT

'Now dear, you really should have told me that you were coming. I'm in no state for visitors.'

'I'm so sorry, Dorothy – may I call you that? – but your agent said he'd checked with you. And it won't take long, I can assure you. Did my editor explain the format to you on the phone?'

Dorothy Daunt sighed. 'I am quite familiar with the "format", as you put it. I read that damn paper every week. What for, I'm not quite sure any more. So, you'll be wanting to look in my refrigerator, I suppose. Let's get it over with.'

With that, she strode over to the ancient, humming Frigidaire that was wedged into the corner of her kitchen below the shelf groaning with yellowing cookery books, and then flung open the door.

Jodie peered inside. In all the weeks she'd been doing this feature for the paper, she'd never seen a fridge so empty – or so ancient, come to think of it. One hunk of crumbly Cheddar, extra mature by the whiff of it, untidily wrapped in greaseproof paper. A box of six large eggs, free range but not organic – three left, but well past the sell-by date, she noted. A milk bottle (a proper glass one, left by the milkman, with a blue foil top – she didn't realise they still sold blue top milk), half empty. The dregs of a carton of double cream. Something fishy, also wrapped in greaseproof paper, which Jodie didn't care to investigate. She couldn't stand fish. A few radishes and cherry tomatoes, unbagged, languishing in the salad drawer, and lastly, half a dozen miniature tonic bottles lined up in the door. '*Alcoholic?*' Jodie scrawled in her notebook.

'What a lovely tidy fridge!' she said brightly to the tall, formidable figure in cardigan and slacks who hovered in the background of the small, old-fashioned kitchen. 'You should see mine! Overflowing with Diet Cokes and Cheesy Dippers, with a couple of ready meals from Aldi to see me through to Friday, when Jason gets a takeaway. Can't cook, me!' She laughed nervously. Why did she say that? All credibility had gone out the window now.

Dorothy, meanwhile, shuddered inwardly. Why on earth had she agreed to this? This reporter woman clearly knew nothing about food. Why couldn't they send someone who at least knew the difference between quince and quinoa? Who could actually follow a recipe, whether it had four or twenty ingredients?

She knew damn well, of course, even if she wouldn't admit it to herself or anyone else, exactly why she had agreed to the interview. It was her last hope. Six years of being the country's top cook (well, one of the top *female* cooks at any rate) and then suddenly her style of cooking had seemed so passé. Too much cream and red meat, too stodgy and too full of calories. Too much bread! All those carbs! Or so they had said in the reviews. But there was more to it than that, surely. What about Delia? Nigella? Mary Berry? Their recipes weren't exactly gifts to dieters. What's more, you still saw them on television, still spotted their new recipe books in Waterstones, piled up high near the till, and still read their interviews in the Sunday supplements. Their books still topped the non-fiction charts. Well, maybe Delia's star had waned quite a bit – and Nigella's, come to that – but then they had other interests now. A football club! The very idea! Dorothy gave another shudder.

Her own face didn't fit any more. That was the reason, she was sure of it. No one had actually said anything, but she was just too old-fashioned, too old full stop. Mary Berry was older than her, true, but she'd had that *Bake Off* series on television that had been so popular. Even Dorothy had found herself watching it, if only to gawp at the ridiculous, over-the-top culinary creations conjured up. Using a whole day's worth of calories on a single slice of cake (not that Dorothy had ever bothered calorie counting. In her view, you should be suspicious of slim cooks.) Mary Berry was a National Treasure these days, so they said. She gave an inward *harrumph* of frustration.

It was all so different now. Cooking had changed immensely since she started out at the Valerie Wilkes' School of Cookery for Young Ladies in South Kensington back in the 1950s. There, she had learned such essential skills as the correct way to position the silverware for a dinner party, and how to fold a napkin in ten different ways.

Back then, you did cookery classes and possibly a secretarial course to pass the time after your O' levels, before you found a husband in a nice safe, secure profession. Only Dorothy had never found a husband, citing a range of excuses to herself – she had no time, couldn't be bothered, cats were less trouble. And she loved to cook, whether it was a cosy dinner party for eight at home or a grand function with waiters bringing out endless canapés and topping up delicate stemmed, crystal glasses that twinkled in the candlelight. In those days, she had had plenty of friends, eligible young men and glamorous girls who had gradually paired off.

The voice inside her head, the one that Dorothy thought she'd managed to suppress after all this time, came back to her. *Shame you didn't find an eligible bachelor to marry. All these years, you've had to get by on your own, and now the money's dried up. Now you're going to have to give up shopping at Waitrose because your pension's not enough. You've spent all the proceeds from your book and there's nothing left.*

Her old editor, Suzanne, had been very nice about it. Suzanne was moving to a new department in the publishing house – crafts not cooking, she'd said – so, of course, she couldn't take Dorothy with her. She was sure she would understand. They were bound to take on another editor who'd contact her in due course, and get her started on another book, since the last one had been so successful. It was only a matter of time, so her old editor had said. But Dorothy's contract had been just for that one book – there were no lucrative tie-ins in those days, no merchandising opportunities – and why would they want to publish recipes from a has-been? *For that is what I am. An old has-been.*

The months had turned into years and still, they didn't contact her. Dorothy was too proud to contact the publisher and beg for another contract, and anyway, she was certain that they wouldn't have given her one. She didn't want to demean herself by contacting rival publishers, either. So she got by doing catering work for a high street shop in the seaside town where she was living on the South Coast and making the odd birthday cake. It was mundane quiches and chocolate brownies nowadays, not intricate six-course meals for star-studded functions. Then again, cooking was cooking and she still loved to do it.

When her mother had died she had inherited an amount of money – not large, by any means – but enough to supplement her earnings, for a while at least. Her lifestyle had taken a dive, though, once the work had dried up. It had been particularly bad in the last few months, what with the recession and fewer orders from the café that employed her. People were still having birthdays, for goodness' sake – she supposed they were just buying everything from the supermarket now. She wouldn't be surprised if the café closed for good soon.

That was why the girl from the paper had found her fridge to be so empty. This was no time for extravagance. Dorothy was simply being frugal, just like everyone who had been brought up during the War. One small chicken could last for four meals if you were careful, while the bones made wonderful stock. Sell-by dates were there to be ignored, obviously, and Tupperware boxes were your friend, not a source of mirth.

And it wasn't as if anyone came round any more. The days of her famous supper parties, with tables groaning with salmon mousse and raspberry roulade, a different wine for each course, were long gone. So were most of her friends, if truth be told, although Dorothy had always prided herself on not relying on anyone. She had been quite close to her brother in Southampton but he had died the year before, leaving her with no close relatives. Heavens, she wasn't even a Godmother!

At least she was getting paid for this article. Not much but not to be sniffed at either. God knows, she needed the publicity. Maybe she'd get another article out of it. The local paper would be interested, certainly, but she wasn't sure if they paid anything at all. Probably not. Still, she could mention it to the owner of the café. And while she was at it, she might mention this other business to the national's Editor – not to this dippy girl who didn't know one end of a turkey from the other. *Yes,* she thought, as the reporter cast her eye over Dorothy's much loved, scruffy kitchen, *once this ghastly interview's out of the way, I'll phone up the Editor chappie and tell him about the notebook. See what he makes of it.*

* * *

A year later

'Look over here, Dorothy. That's right. Lovely. Nearly done now. Just a couple more shots of you holding the book open, with the recipe that sparked it all off. Marvellous! Just tilt your chin up slightly' (*to hide the double chin*, he could have added, but didn't) 'and turn your head towards the window. Super! Bet you never thought it would be this huge, did you?'

'*No*,' thought Dorothy, '*I certainly did not.*'

When she had time, which was not often these days, she would think back to the previous year, just before she had been interviewed about the contents of her fridge for the national newspaper's colour supplement. Up in the loft of her cottage, she had been going through boxes to see what she could send to the church bazaar. She didn't venture up there very often as she was rather afraid of climbing the rickety ladder. If she had fallen or had one of her turns, no one would have found her until the cleaning lady turned up on Friday. (Having a cleaner was a luxury that Dorothy couldn't really afford, but as she always said, one had to have some standards.) In fact, the last time she had gone up into the loft could well have been for the Diamond Jubilee in 2002, when she had come over all patriotic and searched for some bunting that had last been used at the Silver Jubilee in 1977.

Anyway, once she'd made her way up there, Dorothy had lifted up a dusty groundsheet and underneath found a large cardboard box, somewhat dented, its lid tied on with string. Beside it was a battered old trunk with her mother's initials, H C E S. Hilda Cynthia Elizabeth Smyth. This was before she'd married Dorothy's father, obviously. Dorothy only had hazy memories of Frank Daunt, as he'd died when she was young. Having survived military service in the Second World War, he'd been inconveniently killed shortly afterwards while popping out to buy a newspaper, by an out of control bus careering down the High Street. She remembered him as a tall, pipe-smoking man with a moustache, wearing a dark suit and Homburg hat, with very shiny shoes. He would twirl her round and round when he came home on leave.

After his death, the family – Dorothy, her mother and older brother – had moved to Hampshire, to a small village where Mrs Daunt had found employment teaching in the little primary school. Although they were by no means well off, they were lucky that Dorothy's mother had inherited a sum from a maiden aunt, which meant that, as long as they were careful, they had no money worries. In fact, there was just enough money for Dorothy to attend the cookery college after leaving school. She lived in digs up in London with another girl on her course.

Mrs Daunt had continued to live in the same house for years, long after Dorothy and her brother had moved out and set up their own homes. The trunk must have been put in Dorothy's attic years ago when she was clearing out her mother's house. There had been so much to do, what with probate and getting the home ready to be sold, that she had just stuffed a few items that she was keeping up there and then forgotten about them. The rest of her parents' belongings either went to charity or the local auction house. Not that they fetched much. After all that palaver of transporting them there, half of the wretched bidders who'd made successful bids for her lots failed to pay in the end. So she'd had to cart a lot of the items back and give them to charity or send them to the dump.

She opened the box first. It was still sturdy, although some insect (or was it a mouse?) had nibbled holes in one corner. Inside, she found – yes! – her father's Homburg. It was rather squashed and the inside greasy with years of hair oil. Underneath that were various items of clothing – an embroidered waistcoat (now embellished with moth holes), a brocade skirt and a cloth cap, also rather moth-eaten. Why had her mother bothered to keep these particular items?

She moved on to the trunk. It wasn't locked, although it took a few minutes to prise open the lid fully, which must have seized up with age. There was an engraved tankard and a delicate silver tea set, very tarnished by now, but that would come up nicely with a bit of polishing. Quite a bit of mainly costume jewellery that had been inherited by her mother from *her* mother. There was a first edition by Rudyard Kipling. Could she sell that to a dealer? She'd have to do some research. Google it, as they said. An old-fashioned, wooden tennis racquet needed restringing. Dorothy dimly remembered playing with it as a child. It had been so heavy she could hardly lift it at first. Lastly, she found a carriage clock – a bit ornate for her taste; otherwise, she would have had it on display.

That was everything. No, wait. As she was about to close the lid of the trunk, something tucked into a corner of it caught her eye. She reached in and unearthed an old notebook made of cheap brown kraft paper, bearing her mother's name on the cover, written in green ink in the familiar, almost calligraphic hand.

The story of what Dorothy found when she idly flicked through the notebook has since been told many times. It was her mother's old handwritten recipe book. Her daughter would recall that she recognised a few of the dishes as being the ones that she and her brother had been fed on in wartime. She remembered how her mother had been ingenious in stretching food rations to conjure up something that was not just tasty, but also nutritious.

Dorothy had put the notebook aside that day – going up into the loft had taken longer than she'd planned, and now she was hurrying to be at the bridge club, her only social activity of the week. Sometimes, she thought she only turned up so that she would not give the others the satisfaction of thinking that she'd gone into an irreversible decline, and turned into a hermit in her little cottage in a faded seaside town, with G&Ts her only companion. Even if, dare she admit it, this wasn't so far removed from the truth.

That notebook, though, kept returning to her head and refused to go away. Simple, homely recipes that wouldn't break the bank – not outstandingly original by any means, but alluring in these modern times now that everyone was once more tightening their belts. Things like faggots – terrible name but really quite tasty and cheap to make. Plum cobbler – you could get the luscious fruit for free if you knew where to look or had the right neighbours, of course. Chocolate truffles that had no chocolate bars whatsoever in them but still tasted divine. Her mother's scribbled notes in the margin: '*Ask Bill for leg end next time! Muslin's run out – use nylons instead (clean!). Ask Mrs B for butter ration (homegrown rhubarb in exchange?).* Even a few rough pencil sketches of how Mrs Daunt wanted the ingredients to turn out. This not only had the effect of bringing the recipes to life, but also brought that whole era to life; a time when cooking was completely different from today's reliance on ready meals and processed ingredients.

In the days to come, Dorothy found the notebook occupying more and more of her thoughts. She even dreamt about the thing. Eventually, she decided to recreate some of the recipes, using ingredients like scrag end of lamb and tripe to end up with results that, in her view, tasted better, and were probably more nutritious, than many of the recipes peddled by so-called 'celebrity chefs' who seemed to have become famous only through 'blogging' and 'vlogging'. Dorothy wasn't quite sure what these terms meant but they sounded ridiculous.

The recipes she tried were meat-heavy, of course, and not exactly 'clean eating'. Both Dorothy and her mother before her had had no time for vegetarianism. 'Good, no-nonsense food' was how she would have described it, and whether it was animal or vegetable – well, what did it matter? As for this trend where people kept declaring themselves to be vegans – well really, what was the point?

One day, when she was in the middle of trying out a recipe for suet pudding, the great idea came to her. The idea, she would tell people later, that would change her life.

The thinking was this: why not republish her mother's notebook, reproducing every scribbled comment in the margin and every sketch? Perhaps she could add a few words about her mother's background as an introduction? And a mention of Dorothy herself, of course, who had once been almost a household name in cooking, a hundred years ago.

She'd just thought of it as a little project to keep her occupied, now that her cooking jobs were drying up. And if she could get a publisher interested, so much the better.

* * *

Well, all that had happened just over a year ago. Her former publisher, having been so reluctant to take her on again, had jumped at the chance of publishing the notebook, saying that retro was 'in' that year. It didn't take long for a book to appear, owing to the wonders of digital printing.

Then she could hardly believe it, but by the following Christmas, Dorothy's idea had turned into the publishing hit of the year. The book topped the Non-Fiction charts in both Waterstones and WH Smith after it featured in national newspapers and magazines. Amazon ran out of copies and it was, apparently, very big on something called Twitter, not to mention Instagram. Dorothy, to her amazement and glee, found her own star rising yet again. Her days were filled with interviews, 'personal appearances' and photoshoots. Before the book her neighbours had hardly spoken to her beyond a shouted 'Morning!' over the fence. Now, she noted with amusement, they seemed so much keener to talk to her, joking, 'Soon they'll be asking you to go on *Strictly*.' Dorothy wouldn't have dreamt of watching that show, but she did know that her finances, once so precarious, were starting to look healthy again. A major supermarket (though not one that Dorothy liked to shop in) now stocked a line of cookware bearing her name. The quality wasn't really up to her usual standards but given the fee they offered her, it seemed churlish to refuse. Perhaps she could finally get her crowns repaired. And perhaps now she really could entertain the idea of moving house. Cheltenham had always appealed.

After years out of the public eye, Dorothy was secretly thrilled by her new status. She liked the recognition, even if trips to the shops now took double the time they should have done, on account of being recognised and stopped for the ghastly craze of selfies. Her publisher had even created a website just for her! Incredible. (She'd only looked at it twice – the publicity people ran it for her.) There was another book in the pipeline – two, in fact – and even murmurs of a TV series, although only on Channel 4, which she never watched on the grounds that you couldn't beat the BBC.

Of course, after all this activity and her newfound fame, it was too late to confess her little secret. She had far too much at stake now. She couldn't admit how she hadn't stumbled across her mother's recipe book at all. The notebook *had* been there all along in the trunk, it's true. She *had* come across it while she was in the loft, going through a box of her mother's things. But the volume had been completely empty, save for her mother's name inscribed on the front inside cover, and an extremely short shopping list consisting of a pound of potatoes and darning needles. Dorothy, who had been recycling things way before it became fashionable – all her life, in fact – had only kept the notebook, at first, to scribble down her own shopping lists.

Then, she'd had a tremendous idea while browsing the cookery titles in her local bookshop one day (she never bought books any more – couldn't afford to – but she liked to look through them for recipe inspiration). The key to her name becoming as well-known as Mrs Beaton, perhaps (although she only thought this much, much later). She had spotted a gap in the market for a genuine cookbook from yesteryear, reproduced with chatty remarks and interesting period details, and perhaps a few sketches, all straight from the pen of the original cook, with an interpretation by Dorothy Daunt too, naturally. And that was the book which had eventually been published, to great acclaim from reviewers. The great British public seemed to like it too – or, at least, an awful lot of mums and aunties were given it as presents, which did wonders for the sales figures, according to her editor. Whether they actually tried some of the recipes was another matter, but frankly, what did she care as long as people bought the book and all the other merchandise?

The truth behind the book, then, was somewhat different from what everyone had been led to believe. Even her editor was blissfully unaware.

In fact, it was Dorothy, not her mother, who had made up all the recipes and written all the lines dashed off in the margin. Mother and daughter always did have uncannily similar, old-fashioned handwriting, but only her brother would have remembered the similarity and by this time, he was dead. Dorothy had always been something of a sketcher, too. She had spent many happy hours in her bedroom drawing still life studies of vases of flowers or bowls of fruit, but since she had shown no one her work (after her mother, who was quite academic, had come in once and barked, 'What do you want to do that for?') nobody knew she actually had quite a talent for drawing. Funny that her cooking had been actively encouraged while art was seen by her parents as an occupation devoid of value.

As she inclined her head once more towards the young photographer's lens and remembered the letter that had arrived that day from her publisher, detailing a rather large sum to be deposited in her bank account, Dorothy thought to herself that there was absolutely no way she could confess now. No way at all.

COMING HOME

Rain. An insistent drumming had been going on for hours. Rain all night long. Rain battering the skylight on the landing. Rain overflowing the gutter outside the kitchen window, spewing water onto the yard. Cobblestones slick with a wet sheen. The noise competing with the cold tap above the sink, which drips precisely every six seconds and has done for as long as anyone can remember. Rain creeping in under the back door, soaking the threadbare old mat until it can absorb no more, forming slippery puddles on the worn linoleum. Rain accumulating in channels down either side of the road outside, throwing up a deluge of muddy spray every time a car sped past.

It is cold in the house. The particular cold of a crisp late October evening, the sort of day when people open their back doors in the morning and smell woodsmoke and autumn and say, 'Shall we turn the heating on today?' When putting on a jumper is no longer enough to stave off the chill. Once the heating is on, though, there can be no going back until the end of spring, and that's months away. In this house, the annual turning on of the radiators always lags behind the rest of the street.

The old clock on the mantelpiece seems to tick extra loud tonight, even above the constant drumming of the rain. He goes into the kitchen and rinses his mug at the sink, the water pipes rumbling into action as he turns on the hot tap. The noise is so familiar now, it's strangely comforting.

Drying the mug on an ancient, faded tea towel, he hears a sound outside, from the street. A woman laughing, then a voice hissing, 'Shhh!'

It's not her. The couple – it must be a couple – walk on, the sound of heels clacking on the wet pavement. A car is approaching, fast. He hears a shriek, then loud laughter. It's just the woman, no doubt drenched by the water thrown up by the speeding car's tyres.

He makes himself another tea – hot and strong, with only a dash of milk, just how he likes it – in his old, chipped mug, then slowly walks back into the front room and carefully lowers himself into the venerable armchair by the fireplace, his gnarled hands pressing heavily on its arms. The chair has seen better days but he would never change it. His fingers instinctively stroke the threadbare patch on one of the arms. No matter. Who is there to see it, anyway? No one comes round these days. Besides, who needs new furniture at his age? He's too old and too frugal. 'Make do and mend,' that's his motto, and has been ever since the War.

He is uneasy. He knows the time must be way past midnight. Past one in the morning. Senses it in his bones. Where is she? She should have rung, at least. She normally rings. He sips the tea that's cooling rapidly in the chillness of the room, then retrieves his book from the little antique wooden table next to the armchair. He's not really in the mood for reading. Maybe he should put on the radio. Listen to Classic FM for a bit. He's not sleepy.

He becomes aware of another sound above the patter of the rain. Feet moving wetly down a path. His path. Then, a key turns in the lock. It's her. Thank God. It's not today, the day he dreads. The day she goes out, then when he answers his Bakelite phone, still hired from BT, the voice is not hers. The day he finds out something awful has happened to her. Not this day, for she is here. She is back. Thank God. He doesn't know what he'd do without her, even if, for most of the time, she's not here.

'That you, Ellen?' he asks, his rapidly beating heart starting to return to normal. Of course, it is. Burglars wouldn't have a key. Anyway, he knows the sound her key makes in the lock. She has a particularly quick way of turning it. He can hear the unmistakeable tones of someone trying and failing to shut the front door quietly emanating from the hallway. She must think he'd gone up hours ago. How could he, when she was out this late in this weather?

He doesn't need a clock to tell him how late it is. He'd noticed the sudden silence, half an hour ago, as his next-door neighbour, a night owl, had switched off the TV. Watching the usual tripe, no doubt. And earlier, the jeers of a group of lads returning from the local pub after its Saturday night lock-in, as they were lurching past his living room window.

He hears her voice. 'Course it's me, who else were you expecting? I was waiting ages for the night bus, thought it wasn't going to turn up. Nearly got drenched but I sheltered in a shop doorway.'

She has burst into the front room, bringing the icy chill of the night air in with her as she collapses onto the velvet-smooth, mustard coloured sofa, jostling for space among the many overstuffed cushions. She brings, too, the smell of London. Of traffic fumes and dirt and bodies.

He leans forward in his ancient armchair, threadbare but still comfy, moulded to the bony angles of his body. The hardback crime novel he had given up trying to concentrate on escapes from the chair and thumps to the floor, his place in it lost.

She yawns theatrically, opening her mouth so wide it seems it will get stuck in that position, lying rather than sitting on the sofa. She wiggles her toes in ecstasy after unzipping and then throwing off the impossibly high-heeled, black leather thigh boots she'd been wearing. They land one after the other by the ledge of the unlit fireplace. She uncoils the emerald-green feather boa that has been festooned around her neck like a vast furry python, draping it over the back of the sofa, where it lurks, an exotic creature waiting to pounce. Finally, she takes off her long black coat which smells faintly of cigarette smoke and a hint of wet dog.

Even from a distance, her breath reeks of the uneasy combination of champagne and garlic. He can also detect a faint whiff of the perfume that she had applied earlier in the night, before she went out. It was his present for her last birthday, bought on her orders. He may have a good nose for smells, but what does he know about perfume?

'God, I'm thirsty, it was baking in there tonight.'

Without waiting to be asked, he levers himself up slowly from the armchair and makes his way into the kitchen, methodically running the cold tap for a couple of minutes to make sure the water is really cold. It is. It always is. He returns with a tumbler of water for her, which he carefully sets down on a mosaic patterned, glass coaster with jewel-like tones.

'So, what was it like? Did you enjoy yourself?' he asks, settling himself down opposite her. 'I want to hear all about it.'

'God, I'm knackered, can't it wait 'til later? It's nearly two in the morning!'

'I want to know now, right now. I've been waiting up for you all night, after all, with just my book for company. Surely, it's the least you can do?' He had been relieved when she got back but now he is annoyed with her. Tired all of a sudden but still annoyed.

She lets out one of her extra-long sighs. 'All right then, I'll tell you all about it.' First, she drains the water in one long movement, shivering briefly from the icy coolness of it, and dumps the glass; not on the side table, but on a teetering, untidy pile of magazines on the floor.

'So, we got there about 10 from Fleur's flat in Clapham. You remember Fleur? The one who used to work for that casting agency. She was the one who'd got us the invites. I know her from way back. It was the usual crowd. So, we were in this museum-type place, yeah? An art gallery or something. Never been there before. It's great. Like a cavern or something. Anyway, they had this fantastic fashion show about to start, really cool. That new model, what's she called? Lydie or Laura or something. She's only about fourteen. Ukrainian but her real name is totally unpronounceable so the agency changed it. Been in all the fashion mags this month. You know the one.' (He didn't, of course.) 'Well, she was wearing this incredible dress made completely out of ostrich feathers, sort of shimmering as they'd sprayed them gold and silver. It came right down to her feet, almost to the ground.

'Oh yes – her shoes! They were so high! The platforms were see-through and it looked like they were made of glass but Fleur said they couldn't be, must have been acrylic or Perspex or something cos they'd shatter if she stepped down too hard. They were really high – 15cm or something? – that's six inches to you. No, probably higher. We were waiting for her to do a Naomi Campbell but she didn't fall over once. She was brilliant, gliding down the runway like she had trainers on or something, doing all the turns perfectly. She got an extra loud clap and I bet it was because of the shoes. Must have practised for ages.

'Anyway, she had this fab purple handbag slung over her arm which looked like a piece of fruit – I mean, it was designed to resemble an aubergine or something but it looked really effective, you know? Sounds disgusting but it looked great, not cheap at all. I don't know how Valencia gets the ideas for all this stuff. I mean, you wouldn't want to wear a piece of fruit on your arm if you were just popping to the shops, would you, not unless you were about twelve, but tonight it looked perfect.

'Then they had this whole section of other models all wearing mauves and lilacs, my favourite colours. Could have been designed just for me! Shame about the prices. We still get freebies but not nearly so much as we used to. Should have moved to America while I still could, shouldn't I? Instead of staying here with you.'

There is no reply from the armchair.

She gives a half-laugh and carries on. 'Just kidding! I wouldn't leave you on your own! You know I wouldn't! Anyway, this bag was sort of iridescent purples that changed colour when the strobe lighting hit it from different directions. Fantastic. The whole show was fantastic. Wish I could afford it all when it hits the shops! Even the ready to wear will be hundreds of pounds for one item. In my dreams, right?

'Oh yeah, and Bea was there – just got back from the Stein show in New York but she claimed she wasn't jet-lagged. Said it will kick in tomorrow or something. She ate nothing on the flight, just drank kale and beetroot smoothies. Well, that's what she said, anyway. Have you seen the size of her recently? Well, she's not a size six any more, shall we say. Mad as ever though. She was wearing all black as usual but she had on this amazing necklace – it was a leather thong with a leopard's paw on the end. I thought it was a *real* animal paw but when I got up close she let me touch it and it was just an *engraved* leopard's paw on a pebble, all smooth but painted so it looked furry. Amazing! I really want one of those but it must cost a fortune. Probably weighs a ton too, now I come to think of it. Not great for your neck. Bet it will be in the magazines next month. If they send us a sample for the photoshoot, I'm having it. Definitely. Even with a sore neck, it'd be worth it.

'Oh, and I haven't told you about the food! They served canapes before we all went into the show and I wasn't going to have any because we'd had a sushi delivery at Fleur's already and I was really full, but I did anyway as everyone else was, and they were amazing. They had one where all these tiny dishes looked like jewel boxes, but you could actually eat them. Eat the boxes, I mean. Then inside, they had things like mounds of pomegranate and chia seeds and toasted almonds and coconut, and something else but I couldn't work out what it was. Tasted divine though. And they served champagne and other fizzy stuff out of these massive goblets, really tall and thin and all made out of magenta glass cut into facets so they were sparkling different colours when you turned them around. They were quite heavy and we had to be careful they didn't topple over. I was worried mine would smash, yeah, but I wish I'd kept my glass and brought it home now. I could have popped it in my bag when no one was looking. Probably worth quite a bit.

'For dessert, everyone was given this dinky pot of jelly. I reckon it had vodka in it but Fleur swore she could taste something else. These jellies were decorated with lots of nasturtium and pansy flowers and the waitress claimed they were edible but I left mine just in case they weren't. They were too pretty to eat, anyway. I took some photos at different angles, they looked so good. You know, for Instagram.

'Then, finally, at the end of the show Valencia herself turned up – she strode down the catwalk with a model on each arm. My God, she looks ancient now! And she's really petite. Must be at least sixty but she can't be more than a size six. Her feet are so tiny! Like a doll. She had these dainty little bootie things on with tassels down the back. She was wearing this really long, midnight blue velvet gown with about ten animal skins dangling from it, and then these boots just peeping out. Luckily, she had the models to hang on to. She looked like she might slip up at any moment.

'Oh, and she had this amazing hairdo which was as tall as your forearm. I suppose she wanted to give herself more presence, elevate her status. It was kind of backcombed, silver streaked with purple. I thought it was real but Bea said it was a wig and then when she got close to us, you could see she had loads of weavings as well. I reckon she'll have bald patches when she takes the extensions out. I've seen that happen to people on YouTube. There was a whole programme on TV about it and Bea said it had happened to her cousin.

'So, I forgot to say that we were allocated the fourth row when we arrived which is, like, the back of beyond. Virtually the last row. And we were the oldest ones there by miles, I swear. But there were some empty seats, so we waited until the lights went down and then snuck up to the second row. Result! We even had the photographers approaching us to take pictures in case we were famous! It was hysterical! We had to tell them our names at the end and which magazine we worked for. It'll be funny if any of them are published.'

She gives another great yawn. 'I'm really tired now and I've got to work tomorrow, remember? That photoshoot in Leeds. Time to go up. You turn out the lights. I have to use the bathroom right now before I burst. You all right, Dad?'

He grunts but she isn't really interested in the answer. She clomps up the stairs and soon the familiar sounds of running water can be heard from the bathroom, then the flush of the cistern. The boiler groans with the effort of it all. The bathroom door opens, footsteps sound on the floorboards and another door creaks open and shut.

Silence again. At last, the rain has stopped. Nothing moves in the house, save for the second hand of the clock inching around the dial and the drip of the tap. He sighs. Feeling on the floor for his book, he rises heavily yet again from his armchair. Repeating the ritual he has carried out every night for the last twenty years, the old man methodically, automatically, counts the number of footsteps he needs to reach the stairs. Then, gripping the bannisters tightly, a hand on each rail, his sightless eyes staring straight ahead, he slowly feels his way upstairs to his bedroom.

WENDOVER STREET

It had been spring when Charlotte moved into Wendover Street, a thoroughfare of Victorian terraces of the type ubiquitous to South West London. When she had moved into her 'two up, two down' back in April, it signified a real change in her lifestyle. She'd just split up with Matt, who had been unofficially sharing her room in the shared house in Putney for the last few months. It felt right to start afresh. Besides, if she hung around waiting for the right man to build a life with, who knew how long that would take? She was 32 now but saving for a deposit on a house was never going to happen, the way prices were spiralling ever upwards and out of her reach.

So she made the decision to move a bit further out of London, until she was almost – but not quite – in suburbia. That meant she could afford to rent a little house within walking distance (just) of the station. She tried not to think about the crippling price of the season ticket to work. The cost and upheaval of moving would be worth it to put Matt behind her and start a new chapter in her life.

It was the day of her move, a lovely spring morning when you could smell the sweet blossom on the trees, the sun had decided to make an appearance from behind the clouds and the prospect of summer and warmer days no longer seemed an unlikely proposition. The perfect day, in fact, to make a new start.

Charlotte had picked up the keys from the estate agent and her hired Aussie 'man with a van' had just left after depositing her belongings in a sprawling heap on the living room floor. Charlotte had time to look around the house properly for the first time. She'd only had a brief look when the agent had shown her round, then spent almost no time considering whether it was the right place for her, seeing as houses like this got snapped up so quickly. In fact, she'd hardly said goodbye to the agent when she was on the phone to the agency to say she'd take it.

Now she was in, and it was hers – well, for as long as she was paying the rent, anyway. If things got tough moneywise she could always advertise for a lodger, or perhaps let a room through Airbnb. There were always possibilities.

Charlotte put down the armful of clothes she was starting to sort through. She should have thrown some of this stuff out before she moved in.

She wandered through the house. *Her* house. A spare bedroom! A garden! All those things she'd always longed for but never had since moving out of her parents' house after uni at the age of 21. She even had an attic now. Charlotte hadn't ventured into it yet but she pictured a dusty yet useful space where she could store (hide?) her multitude of things collected over the years.

All those craft projects started and never finished. The sketches she'd done at life drawing evening class after work, when she'd fancied herself as an artist. The cardigan that she had begun when she'd started going to the weekly stitch and bitch sessions, given up after three attempts. The mauve silk ballgown was worn once at university, then never again. Charlotte had loved the dress so much, she'd kept it out on display in her room, only to see the material fade. She couldn't bring herself to throw it away, though, because it reminded her of her first serious boyfriend. The keyboard she'd spotted in a junk shop and tried to play for a week before giving up, resigned to the fact that she'd never be a musician. The 'bargain' cat carrier, bought on impulse for £1 in a junk shop, despite the fact that she'd never owned a pet in her life. Well, except the hamster four of them had shared at university in the third year. It had disappeared under the floorboards of their student accommodation in the second week and never been seen again.

Charlotte found she was happy with the idea of continuing to rent. Her mother fondly hoped she would meet a suitable man, pool their deposits and buy a house near the family home in Godalming. Minus Matt, Charlotte was enjoying the single life and in no hurry to put down permanent roots.

It was nice to have a place of her own at last, though. She looked around the large living room, which the owner of the house had knocked through so that the ground floor was no longer three rooms but two. She'd have to buy more pictures now. Still, maybe she *should* advertise for a lodger? No, not yet – she didn't want to go back to having to queue up for the bathroom every morning. Labelling all your possessions, even a half eaten pot of yoghurt in the fridge? Piles of washing up to be done before you could see the worktop? Arguments over whose turn it was to put out the bins? She'd left all that behind now that she had a permanent job in marketing with Rich & Co that allowed her to finance a place which she could call home.

A few members of the older generation still lived in Wendover Street. One or two of them had even been born in the houses there. The day Charlotte moved in, a woman considerably older than her had shuffled out of the adjoining house and called to Charlotte through her still open front door. 'Ida, dear, Ida Tench,' she'd said, while the street's newest arrival was hauling IKEA cardboard boxes along the narrow hallway.

Charlotte, busy with moving, didn't pay much attention to her new neighbour on that first occasion. She had a hazy impression of someone short – maybe five foot tall – with steel-grey hair in an old-fashioned helmet perm, with a yellow duster in her hand. It was that yellow duster which would announce Ida Tench's presence in the weeks to come. The sash window would shoot up noisily, a hand would emerge and the duster would be vigorously shaken out for quite some time. There was a little dog, too, a cute Miniature Schnauzer, who would worm his way round Ida's legs and shoot out the front door, coming to sniff Charlotte's proffered hand. He was called Vinny and his pepper and salt coat was exactly the same shade as Ida's hair. In fact, his luxurious beard reminded Charlotte of Ida's somewhat whiskery chin.

'He's only looking for food again,' his owner would laugh, 'but look at the tummy on him already.'

* * *

It took Charlotte quite a few weeks to get the house straight. She wasn't allowed to decorate as such but she pinned up new curtains and decided to risk knocking a few nails into the walls so that she could hang her collection of holiday photographs and arty posters from exhibitions she'd been to in London over the years. She even tackled the garden, which didn't look like it had been weeded for years – much to the amazement of Gavin and Anoushka, the young couple on the other side of her house at number 34. Horticulture wasn't really Charlotte's thing but she pulled up a few plants that she didn't like the look of, and even planted some geraniums in a terracotta pot that she'd spotted at the DIY store when she was meant to be searching for a floor mop and a laundry bin.

Weekends saw her hurtling off to IKEA in her little baby blue Fiat in search of rugs, frames and more kitchenware. She'd had those things in the shared house, but moving into a home all her own gave her an excuse to buy more accessories – 'you need to personalise the place', as her mother had said when she'd turned up unannounced one day just as Charlotte was going out.

* * *

July, and finally the promised summer had arrived, hotter that year than people had ever experienced. Everyone said so. All conversation was dominated by the heat. It became obligatory, when popping into Sonny's corner shop at the end of the road for a pint of milk, to spend a few minutes exclaiming how hot it was, to which Sonny would solemnly agree. 'Never had anything like it,' he'd say while he counted out your change. 'Global warming, innit? Still, we'll miss it in winter, eh?'

Wendover Street came alive in the heat. Children raced up and down the road, on bikes, scooters and skateboards. Adults emerged to wash dusty cars, water thirsty plants in front gardens and chat to neighbours about the soaring temperature. Cats of assorted colours sunned themselves on windowsills or lounged about on the pavement, inviting passers-by to give them a stroke, occasionally batting a paw at a passing insect. Charlotte had wondered if she should get a cat herself, seeing as she already owned a carrier, but decided that she wasn't home enough.

The heatwave was into its third week now, with no sign of coming to an end. People had given up checking their phones for the hourly forecast, given up turning on the ten o'clock news to see if the hosepipe ban had been lifted. The shops had run out of ice cubes, bottles of water and ice lollies; everyone was being encouraged to save water. 'Check up on your elderly neighbours,' said the newspapers, and 'Don't set off on a trip without a water bottle for each person.'

Charlotte liked the heat. She had worked as a rep in Ibiza once, all summer long, during one of her long university holidays. Still, Ibiza was one thing. South West London, with its humidity and pollution, and a population vastly unprepared for very hot weather, was quite another. She could hardly come to work in tiny shorts and flip-flops, tempting though it was. She put up with the stifling morning train journey to work each day but coming home was the worst, with sweaty commuters invading her personal space and moaning into their phones about the heat and the traffic fumes. If someone started fanning themselves with the free evening paper, Charlotte found herself inching the tiniest bit closer to them in a desperate attempt to benefit from the slightest breeze.

Travelling by train was like sitting in an oven. What made it bearable was the knowledge that she could come back to her own little garden in the evening, a ready-mixed cocktail at hand, and relax in the small patch of shade thrown by next door's apple tree. From time to time, she would see Mrs Tench, always from a distance, usually engaged in some sort of cleaning task – mopping her steps, shaking the duster or vigorously wiping the windows from the inside. Funnily enough her neighbour didn't seem bothered by the heat. Charlotte had barely spoken to her since she'd moved in, partly owing to her working hours, which meant early starts to catch the train and late evenings in the office, quite often followed by going out for drinks with her colleagues or with old friends from university who were also working in London.

* * *

It was early on a Saturday evening and for once, Charlotte had nothing to do. There was no party to get ready for and she didn't fancy watching a film. She was lying on the lounger as the sun was going down, eyes closed, soaking up the last of its rays, thinking that she really should make it to the corner shop to buy some more milk and fizzy drinks. In London, even the outer reaches, it was never what you'd call quiet. She could hear the sounds (and smell the smells) of a barbeque, probably coming from the student house three doors down. A baby was grizzling out of an open window and a horn beeped twice from the nearby main road, followed by someone shouting.

She shifted on her lounger, her skin sticky where it had been pressed into the fabric. She'd taken a magazine out with her but wasn't in the mood to read. It was nice just lying here, with nothing pressing to do. Gradually, another noise came to her from over the fence on the Tenches' side. A faint scraping sound like a spade being dragged across rock. Surely, no one could be gardening in this heat? She opened her eyes but the sound had stopped. She still, though, felt a human presence nearby.

The day before she had come home from work and had the sensation of being watched from the front window of number 30. When she glanced across though, she could make out nothing except a slightly swaying net curtain.

The next day, Sunday, Charlotte was outside in her garden again, luxuriating in the space all to herself, even if it was little more than a backyard. A high fence separated the gardens but she could hear a sound coming from next door again – this time a sort of clicking noise at regular intervals. On impulse, she decided to stand on tiptoe and poke her head over the wall. She was startled to see an elderly man, about her own height, delicately pruning a rose bush, neatly separating branches before giving each one a deft snip and putting the leftovers into a trug basket. He looked too old to be the gardener.

'Hallo,' Charlotte called. The man slowly turned his head round, a bit like a tortoise, to find the source of the noise. 'Hallo,' she said again. 'I'm Charlotte.' Having located the owner of the voice, the man ponderously moved forward in her general direction. He was wearing a stained raincoat that had definitely seen better days, a threadbare flat cap and ancient Wellington boots. 'Ah, err, Horace Tench,' he said, with a touch of reluctance. 'You've met Ida.' It was a statement, not a question.

'Lovely weather, isn't it? Still a bit hot though,' Charlotte said brightly, desperately trying to think of something to say. But the old man had turned away already, back to his task. So Ida *was* married after all. Charlotte had assumed she was a spinster. Strange that she hadn't seen Mr Tench before, especially as she'd lived in the road for months now. Mrs Tench had never given any hint that she was married, and Anoushka and Tom on the other side hadn't mentioned him, but then they were away a lot, on work trips or exotic holidays.

It did seem a little odd, though, that Mr Tench should be wearing a coat and wellies in the hot weather.

Charlotte knew that older people could feel the cold, but surely he must be boiling?

In the weeks to come, when she was talking about her neighbours to her London friends, Charlotte could never bring herself to use their first names. It didn't seem right, somehow. And anyway, clothes aside, there was something a little… *odd* about the pair. She couldn't put her finger on it but they seemed mismatched, somehow. *Is it true what they say about couples? How as the years pass one looks more and more like the other,* she mused. *Like dogs and their owners?* She was not sure it applied to Mr and Mrs Tench. The wife, when she did appear, seemed a larger than life presence. Her husband seemed to fade into the background – on the few occasions that Charlotte caught sight of him after that first encounter over the fence, he was always disappearing inside the house or pulling a curtain closed.

After a few weeks, in fact, she never saw him at all. Mrs Tench would be as active as ever, out dusting as if her life depended on it or polishing the already gleaming door knocker so hard it must surely have some dents. She seemed to have put on a bit of weight and looked more like a ball than ever. In the evenings, when Charlotte was back from work, she often heard the strident tones of the *Coronation Street* theme tune emanating from next door, but she never saw her neighbours once dusk had fallen. Their dog, too, who surely resembled Mrs Tench far more than her husband did, was never to be seen. She'd thought she heard him barking once but that had been weeks ago.

Then one day, the postman arrived uncharacteristically early, as Charlotte was rushing to get to work. Armed with a large, funny shaped parcel, he rang the Tenches' doorbell. The front door opened a crack, then widened to admit the package. Charlotte called a quick 'Morning!' as she set off down her path, glancing behind her. Ida was looking well, she thought – in fact, behind her pinny, she was positively glowing with health. She seemed even plumper than the last time Charlotte had seen her, with rosy cheeks, and had a jolly expression on her face as she thanked the postman.

The same could not be said for Mr Tench. Days later, Charlotte encountered him by chance, for the first time in months. Coming back from the corner shop with a carton of milk, he had nowhere to hide when the two met in the alleyway. His threadbare jacket was hanging off him and he seemed to have some difficulty walking. His face was gaunt and he said nothing as he passed her, just gave a kind of grunt. Charlotte, rushing out to catch a film at the cinema that she'd been looking forward to all week, smiled distractedly at him. Then she forgot about the episode.

* * *

Wintertime, and memories of the summer heatwave seemed as insubstantial as a dream. *Did it really happen?* Charlotte found herself thinking as she came home on the night bus from another evening out in the chillness of the late evening air. There were still plenty of people about, packing the restaurants or walking back from the pub. She'd been having a tough time at work for months now, working really long hours on a new contract. Leaving home at the crack of dawn and coming back late, she hadn't had much time to interact with her neighbours. Charlotte had spent recent weekends visiting her mother, who had come down with some sort of virus that didn't seem to be shifting. She had been dreading her first Christmas without Matt but now she found herself actually looking forward to it because at least it would mean a few days off and the chance for some lie-ins.

Walking briskly down her road, she was about to fish in her handbag for her door key when a movement at number 30 caught her eye. It seemed to have come from the front bedroom. A dim light was on in the room and the curtain was being pulled back slowly. This was unheard of, as normally the thick drapes stayed in place whatever time of day it was. Curious, she slowed her pace, but she didn't want the occupant, whoever it was, to realise that she was watching so Charlotte pretended to rummage for her keys while she risked quick glances up at the first floor.

She could just about make out a figure framed in the window. Surely, that couldn't be Mr Tench? The man, if indeed it was a man, looked ghostly pale by the illumination of the streetlight right outside number 30. As Charlotte watched, he shifted sideways. How thin he seemed. Was he ill? Did he have some dreadful wasting disease? Maybe that explained his reticence to talk to her and the fact that she had only seen him once since that time in the garden. Inserting her key in the lock, she made a mental note to ask one of the other neighbours if they knew what was going on.

* * *

Charlotte loved her attic. Funny how you could exist for years without having something, then once you'd got it, you couldn't do without it. From her student days, she had accumulated masses of stuff that she couldn't bear to part with. Photograph albums of her gap-year trip to India, old revision notes, battered suitcases, tennis rackets, skis, a huge saucepan… everything was up there, out of sight, so that the rest of the house could stay tidy. She had meant to spend some of the summer going through the contents that had been shoved up there the week she moved in. The heatwave, though, had made it impossible. The one time she went up, it had been stifling up there and she'd only lasted a few minutes.

Now it was December already and the anniversary of her move was fast approaching. She decided to have another crack at the attic, mainly to stop her mother constantly harping on about it. What with shopping and lunching with a friend in town, it was late afternoon and the light was already starting to go. The first pile turned out to be her old mathematics textbooks. She'd have to send them to recycling. Next up was a stack of cheap chick lit that she must have taken on holiday once. Time for a trip to the charity shop.

Hours later, she was still going and feeling very pleased with herself for having turfed out so much, although actually it only amounted to a couple of bin bags. There was a laundry bag lurking in the far corner. Charlotte knew it contained ripped jeans from her university days and faded bikinis from her time in Ibiza and long ago holidays. She'd been putting off going through it until now, partly because it contained memories of Matt. But she could delay it no longer.

She made her way gingerly over to the bag, just in case any of the boards were not as sturdy as they looked (as her father had found to his cost when, years ago, he'd first explored the attic in their family house). As she hauled the bag out – now dusty and festooned with cobwebs – she noticed a crack in the bare brickwork behind it which separated her attic space from that of her neighbours at number 30. The crack, caused by a lack of cement between two bricks, seemed to be illuminated and although it was narrow, she found that if she put her eye close up to it she could see right through to their side.

As she'd suspected, there was a light on in their attic too. Strange. It was a lot dimmer than the bare bulb in Charlotte's attic and shed a greenish, slightly eerie glow. Was someone up in the Tenches' loft, then? She took another look.

At first, it was difficult to make out anything but when her eyes had got used to the gloom, Charlotte could see that it was not really an attic after all but a proper, furnished room. Odd, because she could have sworn that there were no windows in the roof when you looked from outside, just like her house. In fact, Charlotte's house and the Tenches' were almost the only ones left in the street that hadn't had their lofts converted. Nearly everyone else had added a third, and in some cases fourth, bedroom. It would probably be the basements next.

She looked through the crack again. Some instinct made her hold her breath. She could make out a door at the far end of the room, some sort of patterned carpet on the floor – it was difficult to see clearly because the light was so dim – then an exceedingly large wardrobe that extended right up to the ceiling. Next to that was a huge brass bed, plumped up with fat pillows. Wait a minute, there were two shapes in it. Two human shapes. Charlotte pressed her eye closer to the crack. Surely, it was Mr and Mrs Tench? What were they doing sleeping up in a loft with no windows, especially on a cold night like this when they could have had either bedroom on the first floor?

Her eyes were gradually adjusting to the gloom, and more of the scene was revealing itself by the minute. Mrs Tench – it was definitely her, no one else could have made that ball shape – was snoring so loudly that Charlotte could hear it on the other side of the wall. She was lying on her side, wearing a voluminous flannel nightgown which nevertheless showed the shape of her huge, distended stomach. The sheets had been thrown off and the garment was hitched up, rather grotesquely, to reveal a large expanse of white thigh, crisscrossed with bluey-purple veins. She seemed to have grown even bigger since Charlotte had seen her last, and now looked hideously obese.

The other figure had to be Mr Tench. Clad in faded pyjamas, which could have been red once but appeared pink in the ghostly light, he looked as if he would break if his wife should roll onto him, his brittle fingers gripping the mattress even in sleep. He seemed to have shrunk to almost nothing; skeletal, like an anorexic, with a wizened head that looked over-large for his body.

I was right, thought Charlotte. *He's definitely ill. Why didn't she mention it? Why hasn't anyone mentioned it? Does anyone else know?* She wished she'd made time to speak to her neighbours. Surely, someone must know what was going on?

The scene was, frankly, disturbing. She was just about to look away when a tiny glimmer of blue light caught her eye, coming, she thought, from between the two sleepers. Static electricity, perhaps? Then she noticed something else. What was it? She peered into the gloom, trying to concentrate. There was a thin tube poking out of Mrs Tench's nightgown, snaking down her gargantuan thigh, curving and disappearing into the gap between her husband's pyjama top and bottoms. It appeared to contain some kind of dark liquid – blood? – with what looked like bubbles travelling in the direction of Mrs Tench.

What on earth? Charlotte moved her eye closer, until her eyelash was actually pressing against the bare brick, to get a better look. Some kind of dialysis machine, perhaps? Whatever was going on in there, the scene was oddly compelling and repulsive at the same time.

She stayed, mesmerised, for several minutes. Then she sat back and let out her breath. What had she just witnessed? No ordinary bedroom scene, that was certain. Something was trying to surface in her memory, something that might explain what was happening on the other side of the wall. The sorting out of clothes forgotten, Charlotte tried to think.

Then she had it. An article that she'd read months ago in a trashy celebrity gossip magazine in the hairdressers. One of their strange medical articles, about the phenomenon of twin to twin transfusion in the womb, where one twin gets stronger while the other gets weaker, quite often ending in death for the sicklier twin. You may have read an article about it yourself.

In that freezing attic room, Charlotte shivered, but it wasn't due to the cold. It was almost as if Ida Tench was sucking the lifeblood out of her husband. She was growing fatter while he had shrunk to almost nothing. No one would believe the unseen watcher, even if she had said anything, and she knew she never could. The idea was surely preposterous. Wasn't it...?

MEMORIES

'Sheila? There's the postie at last. He's turned up so late today, it's nearly the afternoon! I'm going to get the mail.'

Ernie Kinross carefully folded up his broadsheet newspaper and placed it on the already precarious pile of papers, cards and scribbled notes beside him. He got up stiffly (after a couple of false starts) from the old armchair, nearly stepping on a plump, snoozing tabby in the process, and plodded determinedly out into the hall, collecting a battered Tesco Bag for Life from the hook on the back of the door as he went past. A few minutes later, a grunt came from the hall, signifying that Ernie had bent down agonisingly slowly to pick up the post.

Then he was back for another bag, this time a faded pale blue canvas one with grimy handles, one side bearing the word 'Margate'. 'Always more at the weekend,' he muttered, before steadying himself upright and moving into the adjoining dining room with its original fifties dining table and ornate carriage clock on the fifties sideboard.

'Right. Here we go again.' He sat down heavily at the table, elbowing a space among the newspapers, till receipts and advertising flyers, before tipping out the contents of the first bag. A torrent of catalogues, leaflets, brown envelopes and free samples was soon covering most of the available space. Some skittered across the table and onto the floor.

'Bin, bin, bin, bin… here's a postcard from your sister – Majorca is it? Again? – bin, bin, bin… *Another* brochure? They only sent us one last week. What do we want with a blasted conservatory?'

'And what's this one here? An electric car? What's the point of that?' He picked up another one. 'A stairlift? What about the cost? They never tell you that in the adverts, do they?' Grumbling away to himself, interspersed with heavy sighs, he methodically worked through the rest of the post, keeping to one side only the postcard. His wife, meanwhile, a trim, silver-haired lady of almost the same age, put her head around the door. She was wearing a bright red mac and carrying a capacious handbag, while through the door you could see a tartan shopping trolley.

'Just off to the shops, Ernie. I'll be back to make lunch. Just the usual. Bye then.' Ernie barely acknowledged her as he continued to sift through the leaflets, then hauled over the second bag and did the same thing all over again, muttering as he went.

In fact, his wife, Sheila, wasn't going to the shops. Well, not at first. She was going for her weekly coffee and bun with Isla, a fellow volunteer at the charity shop on the High Street. It wasn't a big charity and it only had one shop but rehoming local cats was a cause dear to Sheila's heart. In fact, Hercules, the giant, flatulent tabby whom Ernie nearly stepped on several times a day, had come from the very same charity. Ernie would have preferred a dog but as Sheila had pointed out, who was going to walk a dog every day, what with his hip and her charity commitments? A cat who could come and go as he pleased was much more sensible (although, mostly, he just snoozed in the warmest place, which as often as not happened to be the most dangerous, as it was right next to Ernie's size 14 feet in their ancient slippers. Bathed in the sunlight coming through the French windows, Hercules would normally only wake up for mealtimes – or when he was stepped on, of course. It was a miracle that neither he nor Ernie had suffered a serious accident caused by the other.)

Sheila, meanwhile, briskly made her way down the High Street in the direction of the Cosy Café. As ever, she had a lot on her mind. *Such a relief to have someone else to talk to*, she thought to herself, not for the first time, and that nice Isla was always so understanding. There must have been at least four decades between them but it didn't seem to matter. Isla was always so interested in what she'd been up to. Besides, it was good for Sheila to get out of that house as much as possible. That was why she had volunteered at the shop in the first place. To get away from Ernie. Away from the memories.

Isla, on the other hand, a slim thirty-something divorcee whose apricot nail polish perfectly matched her cashmere cardigan, could think of better ways to spend her time than meeting some old dear who'd become attached to her. This wasn't the first time it had happened, either. There was that Moira, who'd worked in the other charity shop last year. She was on her own and lonely as hell by the looks of it. As soon as Isla had popped her head around the door of the shop to enquire if they needed any help, Moira had made a beeline for her. *It must be something in my face*, she thought as Sheila was chattering about what she'd been up to in the last week.

It was the usual stuff, of course. Gardening, waiting for the plumber who never turned up, the doctor running late again… she was sure that elderly people visited the doctor mainly to have someone to talk to. No wonder the NHS was in such a state, waiting rooms constantly clogged up with worried pensioners.

Sheila was still talking – something about her niece, was it? Isla rearranged her expression and tried to look interested. At their first meet-up, Isla had waited for Sheila to mention grandchildren. They always worked them into the conversation early on, in Isla's experience. Not a thing though. And no talk of children either. Odd. Perhaps they'd married late in life and missed their chance of having any.

Isla herself was currently single although she did have an on-off boyfriend, Dave, who was currently very much off. Dave had made his feelings about children crystal clear. 'If you get pregnant, love, I'm off. My three with Cath are too much to cope with as it is. Another one and I'd have no money left at all. Never should have married her.' So all things considered, it was probably just as well that Isla couldn't stand children and had no intention of having one herself. Cats were different. They didn't have screaming tantrums, for one thing, laying down on the floor in Tesco and wailing while you were trying to choose the vegetables.

Last month, Sheila in the shop had come down with flu. Typical, she herself had said later – it had to happen three days before she was due to pop down to Boots to get the free injection. To get out of doing her shift at the shop, Isla, who was easily bored and also rather nosy, had volunteered to pop round to Sheila's house and see if she wanted any shopping done, seeing as the husband never seemed to leave the house now.

So there she was, walking up the crazy paved drive to the semi. It took a long time for the husband (Ernie, was it?) to answer the door. 'You must be Isla,' said a stooped, white-haired man in a greying cardigan, allowing her in, reluctantly. Inside, it was dark, despite the sunny day, with all the Venetian blinds pulled down and a smell of plug-in air fresheners mixed with something else indefinable. Isla shivered slightly. One day, she'd be that old, if her sins didn't get her first. Isla spotted a framed black and white photograph of a couple on their wedding day, dating from the fifties, it looked like, judging from the dress and the hairstyles.

'What a lovely photo!' she exclaimed. 'You and Sheila, is it?'

Ernie nodded. 'That's right. Nearly sixty years we've been together now. Incredible when you think about it.' *He doesn't sound too happy about it*, thought Isla. He was still talking. 'There's just the two of us. No children.' He repeated it more softly. 'No children. Now, where did Sheila put that shopping list…?'

* * *

A month later, Sheila had fully recovered from her illness and was tucking into a toasted teacake in the little café on the high street. She could have gone into one of the chains – three they had in this town, imagine that? – but she preferred the Cosy Café, which was mainly populated by women of a similar age to herself, sometimes accompanied by reluctant offspring taking their mothers out for a couple of hours. All the teenagers seemed to go into Costa and the rest, taking selfies on their mobile phones and shouting and laughing so loudly you couldn't hear yourself think. Putting their feet up on the chairs – disgusting, she called it.

Proper waitress service here, it was. Now that slip of a girl serving them, Amy she was called, had such a lovely smile, and she always saved an Eccles cake for Sheila. Anyway, she never would have got through a coffee in one of the big-name shops. You asked for a regular cup and when it came it was the size of a swimming pool. Ridiculous. *And* there was far too much choice, in Sheila's opinion. She just wanted a coffee with milk, not one of these ridiculous salted caramel frappe-whatsit things that surely rotted your teeth with every mouthful. Salt *and* sugar in the same drink. Imagine that! Not that Sheila had many teeth left – in her day, they whipped them out so you could get the full set of dentures.

Besides, Isla said she liked the little café, said it made a change. Sheila was enjoying herself. If truth be known, she wished she could talk all day to Isla, rather than having to go home. The talk had turned to her husband.

Isla, on the other hand, was bored and wished she was at home watching the latest baking programme on catch-up.

'I don't know what he'd do without me,' Sheila was saying. 'You've seen him. Never goes out now. Just stares out the window a lot of the time.

'He's wrong, you know. About us being childless. I heard him tell you that time you popped round. We did have a son, once. Alfie, we called him. Lovely wee thing, he was.'

Isla, who had been gazing out of the window and wondering what shade of polish to go for next at the nail bar, suddenly straightened up in her seat and hurriedly put on a concerned expression. *This sounds interesting*, she thought, ever alert to the misfortunes of others.

'What… what happened, Sheila? Would you like to talk about it? I'll understand if you'd rather not, of course I will. You just take your time.'

Sheila paused, then put her teacup down.

'He died. Just like that. No warning. In his cot. I just went in one morning and he was cold. Twelve weeks old. Ernie blamed me, I think, although he never said. He'd been fine when I put him to bed. No temperature, no rash, no sniffle, nothing. And I looked in on him in the night, just before we went to bed, same as usual. Everything normal. He was just sleeping peacefully. I always made sure to see the blanket was moving up and down, so I could tell he was breathing. There was nothing wrong. Nothing at all. Until I came to get him up in the morning and he was just lying there, not moving, cold. His lips were a funny colour – bluish. I tried everything to wake him up but nothing worked. I ran to get a flannel from the bathroom, put some cold water on it, put it on his face. Thought the shock would wake him. Of course, whatever I did, it would have been too late anyway. They told me that later. But I had to try. Had to.'

Her eyes filled with tears and Isla thought the older woman was going to cry. *Not here*, she thought. *Not in the café for God's sake. I can't stand it when people cry.* Isla put a hand on Sheila's arm while she carried on talking.

'Of course, nowadays you have to put the baby to sleep in a particular position, don't you? I read it somewhere. We were never told that then. Not in those days. It was fifty years ago. Didn't have a nanny state like we do now. Nobody talked about "cot deaths" then.

'He never got over it, you know. He tells people we've no children. On forms, he ticks the "no children" box. But we have. We've still got our Alfie. He's still on Ernie's mind. I know because he's with me too. Every day, every hour. He'd be 50 this year. His birthday's next month, you know.'

Sheila was talking so softly now that Isla had to lean forward to hear her. 'That's when I had the idea, you know. To stop Ernie brooding so much. I was all right. I had my job to keep me busy. People to see and have a chat with. Like you. But after he'd retired, he didn't have anything to do. He's never had any hobbies, doesn't like sport. Doesn't even watch telly much. He spends all day thinking about Alfie and nothing else, I'm sure of it. Even after all these years. Brooding. I tried to get him to go on outings – they have coach tours in the local paper, lots of places they go to. Stately homes, gardens… We went on a couple but he was only there on sufferance. I could see he wasn't really there, if you see what I mean. He was back at home with his memories. Waste of money taking him on a trip.' She pulled out an old-fashioned, embroidered handkerchief and delicately wiped her nose.

'So I thought I'd give him something to do. To take his mind off things. Oh, maybe it's wicked of me, but I can't stop it now you see. We're in the system.'

What on earth is she talking about? Isla glanced around the café but thankfully no one else was paying them any attention. The customers were chatting as usual to each other and the waitresses were buzzing about distributing large slices of cake and cups of tea. Whatever the woman had done, when Isla got home she would ring up her friend Lou to tell her. Lou, who'd been to school with Isla, got all her tales from the charity shop – the difficult customers who tried to haggle, the homeless people coming in looking for warmth, the shameless shoplifters.

'You can tell me Sheila, it's OK,' she said in her most confiding voice. 'I won't let on.' *Well, only to Lou.*

Sheila swallowed and gazed in the direction of the steamed up window. 'Well, it's like this. There's no computer at home. Ernie's never touched one. Wouldn't know how to turn it on, let alone use it. Says he's too old to learn now. "What's wrong with typewriters?" he says. He thinks I don't know anything about computers either, but I do. I've been going to classes in the library for months now. "Silver Surfers" they call it. Afterwards, they let you use their machines. You know, for surfing the Internet, writing letters and that.

'Well, I got on quite well with the course. Six sessions it was. All free. The teacher says I'm a natural at computing. I've got my own email address and everything. I've been logging on and registering. On websites, I mean. Where it says, "Contact us," I've typed in our details. Given our address. Even though Ernie's always been so particular about us being ex-directory.

'Then once they know your details, where you live, they start sending you things. Holiday brochures. Leaflets. Free samples. Begging letters from charities. I didn't know how so many people seemed to have got hold of my details, but it turns out that if you tell one company, they sell their mailing lists to others. I realise that now. Ernie would be horrified but it's better for my plan. Ernie gets the mail in every day. I thought, if he would just concentrate on the letters, it might stop him from thinking about wee Alfie for a bit... Maybe he might even agree to go away for a few days, if he saw the holiday brochures. Lovely, they look, some of those places. A little hotel in Harrogate would suit us down to the ground. We just need a change of scene, Ernie and I.

'Well, this went on for a while and for a bit, my plan worked. Ernie was distracted by all the post, all right. But I got a bit... *addicted* I suppose you'd call it. Couldn't stop typing my name into Internet forms. I was in that library 'til closing time once, filling them in. The man behind the counter made a joke of it. Luckily, Ernie never sets foot in there.

'Anyway, we've had to order another two recycling boxes from the Council just to contain it all. It can take him all morning sometimes just to deal with the post. It would have been all right, even then, but I went too far...

'I started subscribing to things. Book clubs. Trial memberships. Magazine subscriptions. It's all free at first, but to get things for free you have to give them your card details.

'We have a joint account, you see. Ernie's not interested in our finances. Leaves it to me to check, ever since Alfie died. He used to be so particular but he can't deal with it now.' She sighed heavily and twisted her slim gold wedding ring, which by the look of it would never again come off her swollen finger.

'Anyway, if you don't want to pay you have to cancel the subscription in time. Only I... I wasn't in time. Not always. Sometimes, I forgot. I'd ordered so many I couldn't keep track. Or you'd have to phone and I couldn't get through. I couldn't use the phone at home, anyway, else Ernie would want to know what I was up to.'

Isla, sipping her coffee while trying to maintain her concerned expression, was stunned. Sensible Sheila... who'd have thought it? This was a turn-up for the books. This was getting interesting. Really interesting.

Sheila was still talking. 'I didn't mean to get in so deep. I just wanted to take his mind off things, away from Alfie for an hour or two. And it worked, for a time at least. But I wish I'd never started it now. You see, it's not just the magazine subscriptions. It's more than that. I've been ordering things... from catalogues. And on the Internet. Amazon, eBay... it's so easy. A couple of clicks. I didn't use our postal address, you see, after the first few things, so that Ernie wouldn't find out. I used the shop. They come straight to me there, the packages. I'm the one who opens up the shop in the morning – got my own key and everything – and the postman's usually early, before the rest of the staff get in. Who's to say it's not donations?

'Then I take the stuff back home. In my shopping trolley, bit by bit, under the vegetables, so nobody notices. And it's piling up in our spare bedroom. Ernie never goes in there. Can't face it any more. It used to be Alfie's room…'

Sheila wrenched her gaze from the window. She turned to look at Isla, struggling to keep her composure. 'So now we're in debt and it's all my fault. I told Ernie some money was missing from our account. I don't know why I told him – it just came out one day when I couldn't keep it a secret any longer, it had been playing on my mind that much. I didn't tell him how much was really missing. He thought someone looked over my shoulder when I was getting out money at the cashpoint on the High Street. He's read about that kind of thing in the papers. He always said I shouldn't use those machines, said I should go into the bank like he does – or used to, when he was still leaving the house.

'He thought it could be sorted out if I just talked to the bank. But it wasn't a stranger who took the money. It was me.

'I told him we were missing £100. That's bad enough. He couldn't believe it. To him, that's a fortune to lose. He doesn't realise inflation's been so bad recently. In the end, I told him it had been sorted out, a clerical error. Just to stop him asking questions.

'The thing is, it's not £100. It's not even £1000. It's more like…' (here, her voice hushed to a whisper) 'thousands. Maybe £10,000. Maybe more. Maybe even £15,000. I can't say exactly. A fortune, whichever way you look at it. And I… I don't want to know the real figure. I can't bear it, Isla. *I just can't bear it any more.*'

Isla let out an involuntary gasp. This was getting more and more interesting. Who'd have thought Sheila would steal from her own husband? For that was what it amounted to, even if she'd never meant to.

Isla's own pilfering of charity shop items seemed insignificant by comparison. She'd joined the shop when staff at her old charity shop, in the next town, had become suspicious that things were going missing. She'd only taken some stuff that people had stupidly left outside before they opened (a sign told you not to do that – couldn't they read?) or things they'd brought into the shop which hadn't been priced up yet. Hardly stealing, was it? Just a few bits and pieces. A couple of novels and a jumper. The black dress with the tiny moth hole that was easily fixed with a bit of darning. Oh, and the nice beaded bag that looked like it had never been used. She'd forgotten about that one. Designer, that was. She could sell it on eBay. Not that many things really. And anyway, the owners clearly didn't want them because why else were they donating them to the charity shop?

Before she could be accused of anything, Isla had stopped working at the shop, confident that no one would pursue her. This time, she chose an independent, one of a kind shop because then it wouldn't be warned by another branch. There was no proof, after all, since the stuff she'd taken hadn't been logged yet. And when she did take something, she wasn't stupid enough to keep it at home. Lou was more than happy to keep things for her, no questions asked, in return for the odd present or two. From the charity shop, naturally. Brand new things that people hadn't even unwrapped, unwanted presents, stuff they'd lost the receipt for and couldn't return to the shop.

Isla saw it as a perk of the job. After all, she wasn't being paid for working there, so why shouldn't she make a bit of cash on the side? No one would ever know. She'd made a mistake with that beaded bag, though. One of the other volunteers had been handed it over the counter and had remarked at the time how nice it was, how they should Google it so they knew what price to charge. She wouldn't try and sell it now until the fuss had blown over. Perhaps in the new year, when she would need to finance a holiday with Dave, once they were back on…

Isla snapped back to the present. Sheila was staring straight out of the window again, her eyes glassy, unfocused. Surely, what Isla's café companion had done was much worse?

Sheila. Sensible, dull, blue-rinsed Sheila. Who'd have thought it?

Sheila was speaking again. 'All the worry… it's making me ill. I can't sleep at night for tossing and turning about what to do.'

'I'm sure you can get help. Citizens Advice Bureau or something?'

Sheila shook her head. 'It's all too much now. I'm too tired to deal with it. I'll have to tell him. Ernie says only death will save him from the avalanche of mail. But it's worse than that. Much worse. If I don't pay the bills they'll increase them. I've already had letters, threatening letters, saying something about a debt collector coming round. A bailiff. The shame of it! What if the neighbours saw? If I can't get the money back, we'll lose the house, I'm sure of it. We paid off the mortgage, but Ernie's only got his tiny pension, and I've never worked. Too busy volunteering for good causes. What will we live on? There's food to buy, and all the utility bills. Council tax. Vet bills for Hercules. We'll have to sell the house to pay our debts. The house where Alfie was born. Then what will happen? What will it do to my Ernie? The shock will kill him, I'm sure of it.'

'I can't believe what I've done. What am I going to do, Isla? It's all such a mess. Such a terrible mess.' Suddenly, she reached across the table and grasped both of Isla's hands, surprisingly tightly for a woman of advanced years, as if her life depended on it.

'*What am I going to do...?*'

THE WRONG CAKE

'Yes, yes, go on. I'm all ears.'

'Well, it was quite extraordinary, Connie, because the thing was—'

'You can't say "quite extraordinary", Barb. Either it was extraordinary or it wasn't.'

'Yes, all right dear, let me finish my story.'

'I'm only saying.'

'*Will* you let me tell you what happened or not?'

'All right, I'm listening.' The trouble with Barbara was that she took ages to say anything.

'Anyway, he'd only been out of the clinic for a week and he was staying at his mother's. You know, Pat with the hair.'

'The purple highlights?'

'No, the other one.'

'So what happened then?'

'Well, nobody knows for sure, but this Pat had a friend, you see, and they'd take it in turns to go to each other's house for coffee. Once a week. So that week it was the friend's turn to—'

'What was this friend's name?'

'Marge, I think it was. Yes, that was it. I've never met her but I've heard talk about her. So she – that's Pat – let this Marge in and they both went into the kitchen while Pat made the coffee. She's got one of those fancy espresso machines now, a bit like you get at Costa, only it takes those funny pod things. Cost a fortune as it's built into her units. Bugger to clean though. S'cuse my French.' Barbara paused for breath.

'Go on.'

'Well, Pat's friend had turned up with some cake.'

'I'm partial to a bit of cake myself, especially homemade. Special occasions only, of course. Got to watch my figure.' Connie patted her sizeable stomach. 'What cake was it then?'

'Ah well, that's where it gets interesting. You see, according to a friend of mine, this Marge would always bring round a pack of Cherry Bakewells. Never homemade. She didn't do baking. Can you believe it?'

'So, she always brought Cherry Bakewells?'

'Always. Now we don't know for certain but I did hear that she was sweet on Pat's husband.'

'*No!*'

'That's what I heard from Elsie. But don't tell a soul because I swore I'd keep it a secret. I've only told you and my friend down the club, and she swore she wouldn't tell anyone except her friend who works at the hairdresser.'

'What's that got to do with Cherry Bakewells, though?'

'Well, Don's partial to them, you see, and it was like a little code between them. Him and Marge, I mean. Or so I hear. Sort of like, she was thinking of him and giving him a little present but Pat wasn't to know. Because, of course, those two didn't finish the whole box in one go so there were always two or three left for Don when he came home from work. Always one for snacks and whatnot, is Don. How he's not the size of a house, I'll never know.'

'Wish I had the same problem, Barb!' Connie involuntarily sucked in her capacious middle.

'Anyway, this time was different. She didn't come with the Cherry Bakewells. She brought round…' (here, Barbara paused dramatically) 'fondant fancies.'

'Sorry Barb, you've lost me there. What have fondant fancies got to do with anything?'

'Just listen to the story, Con, you've always been too impatient. I'll get there in me own time. So, Pat arranges these fondant fancies on a plate, as normal, and brings them through to the lounge. She sits down with her friend and they have a good natter, as usual.'

'About what?'

'Oh, I don't know Con, it's not important. Probably who's carrying on with who, any bargains in the supermarket, that sort of thing. Let me get on with the story.'

'Then what?'

'Well. Pat happened to mention that Fred was home. The son, you know. He's a bit shy and he was upstairs in his room.'

'What was he doing in his room?'

'How do I know? Probably checking his Facebook page, if he's anything like my Neil.'

'Now, as I said, Fred had only been out a week, but Pat's friend didn't know that. The family didn't like to tell people, you know. Didn't want gossip the minute their backs were turned. This Marge – or whatever her name was – well, she was close to Pat but not that close. Closer to Don, if you know what I mean, but even he didn't let on. *I* knew but only because Vera in the hairdresser had told me the week before.'

'But how did it happen?'

'I'm coming to that. Pat nipped off to the downstairs lav, and while she was in there, this Marge thought she'd pop up and sneak a look at Pat's new bathroom suite that she'd been going on about for ages. How much it cost and whatnot. But she didn't want to actually ask Pat to see it because Pat might think she was jealous. Which she was, obviously.'

'Well, of course, she was.'

'Anyway, since Fred was home, she took the plate of fondant fancies up with her, in case she bumped into him. Between you and me, I think she was curious about him too. Wanted to see what he looked like, in case he had two heads or something. Always been nosy, that one. I knew it would get her into trouble in the end. I said to Vera, "That one's too nosy for her own good." And look what happened!'

'So what *did* happen, Barb? I'm dying to know.'

'I'm coming to that. Anyway, this Marge goes upstairs, holding the plate of fondant fancies. They'd eaten four already – Pat had *three*, apparently, although she's supposed to be looking after her figure. And she'd only just joined Weight Watchers again. Not a very good start, was it? So, anyway, there were four of these fondant fancies left on the plate.'

'Go on.'

'Well, she goes upstairs with the plate in her hand, has a look at the new suite – it's got a freestanding bath with claw feet and marble tops, can you imagine? In that little semi? Overdone, if you ask me. When they come to downsize, it'll put buyers right off. You have to climb into it and there's nowhere to put your bubblies. Anyway, she was just coming out when Fred's door opens and he catches sight of her. He's a bit surprised, like, but he says, "Hallo". Or so the story goes.'

'What's this Fred look like, then?'

'Well, I haven't seen him since he was a youngster, but I did hear he'd put ever such a lot of weight on. Anyway, let me get on with the story. So this Marge had just met Fred, and then—' Barbara lowers her voice and theatrically looks round the teashop to check whether anyone else is listening – '*he catches sight of the fondant fancies!*'

Her friend, pausing midway as her pudgy fingers reached out for a chocolate éclair, looked mystified.

'And then?'

'Well, that was it. They said it was his heart. Gave out because of the shock, what with her shoving that plate of cakes practically under his nose without any warning, and him being – I don't mind telling you – obese as it was.'

Connie's upper body flesh rippled in sympathy. 'Who'd have thought it? All because of a dish of cakes. You couldn't make it up, could you?

'I hear the friend never comes round to the house any more. Pat's never forgiven her. Even Don's said they can't meet any more, given the circs. All right, she should never have gone upstairs like that, without waiting for

Pat. Bad manners, that was. Snooping around like that. But how was she to know? She only wanted a look at the bathroom without Pat hovering at her elbow, droning on about the quotes they got and how they tried three different tile designs.

'Bet that Marge can't live with herself now. Probably has nightmares about it.'

'But… I don't understand, Barb. Did he eat one? Did he have an allergy? Because my cousin, you know, gets terrible hives if she so much as sniffs scrambled egg…'

'Allergy? Oh no, dear. You're wrong there. Fred had no allergy to anything. He could eat whatever he felt like. No, it was the colour that did it. Sounds incredible, doesn't it, but I swear it's true. Pat told me herself. The pink fondant on the fondant fancy. There were two yellow ones, one chocolate one and one pink one left. If they'd only eaten all the pink ones before she went upstairs, it would never have happened.

'Fred had a phobia of pink, you see. Not just any old pink, mind you. Your fuchsia pink, or your fluorescent pink – he could cope with those, easy as you like. No trouble. But your bubblegum pink, your blossom pink, your marshmallow pink, or your – well, your fondant fancy pink. They were deadly. Couldn't go near them. Started when he was a boy, apparently. Don and Pat just thought he was being silly, making a fuss. Don't most boys hate pink, think it's girly? Then they grow up and start wearing pink shirts and socks and all sorts.

'But he never grew out of it, and it got worse and worse through his teens. He was hospitalised once, with

140

the shock. By that time going with his mum to the shops was impossible, of course, and they had to stop his little cousin coming round because she loved wearing pink. He couldn't even go near a television that was on, just in case. And in springtime, he had to keep his curtains closed. Too dangerous, you see. Too much chance he'd see a flash of the wrong shade of blossom on the trees and it might tip him over the edge. They had to cut down their lovely cherry tree in case the blossom blew in. I heard they even found him a special filter for his computer that changed all the pink to another colour, so that he could use it safely.'

'Well, what a thing to happen! I've never heard of that before.' Connie, both shocked and fascinated at the same time, was contemplating having the last eclair.

'That's exactly what I said to my Roy, but it's commoner than you'd think, Con, apparently. That's why he'd been in the clinic. Getting cured. Supposedly. They start off exposing you to a tiny flash of the thing that causes the reaction, under strictly controlled conditions. Could be anything you eat, if you have an allergy, or if you're like Fred, just something you catch sight of. Peanuts, spiders, a certain colour… They gradually give you more and more exposure to it until you have no reaction at all. Takes months, apparently, and often years. They must have thought it was safe for him to come home. Didn't do a very good job though, did they?'

'No, you're right there, Barb. They certainly didn't.'

Connie eyed her plate, empty save for a few crumbs. 'Pass me another slice of that Battenberg.'

FANCY THAT

Gerald Hare was a man continually amazed by coincidences. He could find a coincidence in anything. Visiting Rome as part of his annual summer holiday fortnight ('a delightful cultural and epicurean tour' was what he and his wife had actually booked, according to the travel agent's blurb), he bumped into his next-door neighbour in the queue for an ice cream at one of the busy gelateria around the corner from the Spanish Steps.

'Well, fancy seeing you here!' Gerald exclaimed with genuine amazement when his eyes alighted on Martin and his girlfriend from number 27. Whereupon his wife pointed out that she had told Gerald back in January that Anna and Martin were doing a coach tour through Italy that summer, visiting some of the major cities, and didn't he think it sounded like a marvellous idea?

'Would you believe it?' he said a few weeks later, when he spotted his window cleaner, Perry, in Tesco, wearing exactly the same diamond patterned waistcoat as he had been given by his mother for a Christmas present in 1989. Whereupon his wife refrained from telling him that she had taken the very same waistcoat to the Helping Hands charity shop by the bus depot just the week before because she was sick to death of the sight of the thing hanging on the outside of the wardrobe door in Gerald's den, gathering dust, along with a sludge green raincoat he'd had for at least 15 years and never worn either.

Then, the same month, Gerald came back from work one evening and announced, 'I bumped into Arthur on the High Street. Do you know, I never knew his birthday was the day before mine. That's a bit of a coincidence, isn't it? I should take him down the pub to celebrate.'

His wife, who had never liked Arthur much but had known the date of his birthday for a good ten years, which was six months short of the total time she had been acquainted with him, said nothing and got on with ironing Gerald's work shirts.

'Now *that*,' said Gerald excitedly, stabbing a finger at the newspaper over breakfast a month later, 'that is just what I was saying to you yesterday. Remember? About those ridiculous reality TV shows. Funny that there's an article about them, right after my comments. This journalist agrees with everything I've said!'

'It's their job, dear,' said his wife. 'If journalists aren't creating stories out of nothing, they are investigating the subjects that are on everyone's lips. That's what the media does. You only mentioned it because you saw that programme on television the night before. Well, so did a lot of their readers, so the newspaper does a follow-up story about it, because they know there's interest.' She went back to spooning her porridge, a touch smugly, Gerald felt.

He kept silent. Sometimes, he reflected over his mug of English Breakfast, it was rather a bind being married to a university professor of media studies. He rather wished that he had married a woman who wasn't (or didn't act as if she was) his intellectual superior. At the time, he hadn't been worried at all, hadn't minded that his wife seemed to have the lion's share of the brains in their relationship. He was intelligent too. Of course he was. His job as Class Teacher for Year 3 at St Olave's School in the neighbouring town might have impressed some, but held no awe for his wife, who constantly reminded him that her job was more demanding, seeing as she was expected to write papers on her subject that would go on to be published and reviewed by her peers, and also be at the forefront of research into media matters. She was, indeed, often invited to conferences at other universities, even overseas, which seemed to involve lots of free trips to exotic (in Gerald's admittedly limited experience) places, in countries he would never dream of visiting.

Meanwhile, he seemed to be doing crowd control for a living rather than any actual teaching, and the closest he got to travel in his work was when he took the Year 3s along the High Street for their geography project.

The only reason his wife ironed Gerald's shirts was because she knew that if he attempted to do it himself, the inevitable result would be singed fabric and a lingering burning smell, or else he'd forget entirely that he'd left the iron switched on.

Gerald and his wife had miraculously produced one son, Billy, who clearly took after his mother in most things – which was probably a blessing. Seventeen and at college, he was currently on the path to win a place at a very highly thought of university indeed; if he could be persuaded to keep up his diligent studying for just a few more months, that is. His mother had said more than once, 'Well, look at it this way, Billy. Would you prefer to stay at home with your father or would you like to go away to university and enjoy yourself?' He carried on with the studying.

* * *

August, and it was holiday time for every member of the family. There was a lot to be said for the three of them sharing school holidays, Veronica Hare thought; but then again, there was a lot to be said for the three of them *not* having holidays which coincided. One or other of the boys would insist on getting under her feet when she just wanted to catch up on the newspaper or sit down with her tablet and do a quick bit of research on Google. She retreated to her study quite a lot, and not only to work.

Now, it was Gerald racing into the living room, breathless with excitement. 'Look! Look!' he cried, brandishing an envelope. 'Remarkable!'

'What's remarkable?' Veronica replied in a disinterested tone, carrying on with her reading.

'It was in today's post. I've won tickets to that show. You know, the one at the local theatre that opens next week. I won the draw! What are the chances of that?'

'Quite high actually, Dad,' came a voice from the sofa. 'Hardly anyone reads that local rag now that they get all the news on their phones, and the odds of winning a local competition are always more favourable than being lucky in a national one, anyway. Look at that voucher you won last year for the dog racing. You ended up spending loads of money on bets and you didn't win a thing. They're probably desperate to get rid of tickets.'

'Well, I'm going to see the show even if no one else is,' Gerald retorted, a note of petulance in his voice. 'It's next Thursday. The whodunnit. Are you coming with me, love?'

Veronica glanced up from her paper. 'Can't, I'm afraid. Going round to Suzi's.'

'Billy?'

'No chance, Dad. It's not really my thing. You'll have to go on your own.'

'Damn. Oh well, it'd be a shame to waste the chance of a free night out so I might just do that.'

In Gerald's family, nights out were few and far between. Or at least, nights out where Veronica and Gerald went out together were really very rare indeed. She seemed to have a constant stream of committee meetings, reading group nights, film club evenings or meals out with the girls. Gerald, on the other hand, had to make do with occasionally going to the pub with some of his colleagues.

* * *

It was the evening of the performance. Gerald, who had taken more care with his appearance than usual, left extra time to get to the theatre. He backed his car out of the drive while waving to his wife and son. 'See you later,' he said. 'I'll tell you all about it. Just picking up Graham first.'

He'd told his wife that his old friend from college days who lived in the estate up the road was coming along, but actually, he wasn't picking up Graham at all. He'd found a taker for the second ticket all right, but it was Lynn the school secretary, who Gerald had been sweet on for some time. *Let her think I'm being extra generous this time*, he thought to himself as he pulled up outside her flat, which was in the next town. She waved to him from the window then opened her front door, wearing a sparkly black dress with shiny blue high heels. *It's nice to be with someone who just wants to enjoy themselves for a change and not score points off me. Look at that cracking figure!* thought Gerald as he stopped the car.

'You look nice, love,' he said as he opened the car door for her. 'Hop in.'

The play was not really Gerald's thing at all. It was a creaky whodunnit, rather dated, starring a couple of has-beens from television sitcoms that he vaguely remembered from his younger days. Lynn probably hadn't been born when they were household names. The scenery was all aspidistras and grandfather clocks, and looked a bit battered from being wheeled out at countless provincial theatres while on tour, no doubt. Still, the theatre was surprisingly packed and they had good seats (albeit a bit of a squeeze to fit your thighs into) in the circle, second row from the front. Lynn seemed to be enjoying herself anyway, tittering at the occasional jokes and acting scared when the music went all spooky and the lights dimmed. Gerald risked putting his hand on her knee and she let him keep it there. He was having rather a good evening. The best evening he'd had for a long while, in fact.

The curtains closed on the cast and the lights went up to announce the interval. As everyone around them stood up gratefully to stretch their legs – it was an old theatre and the seats were definitely rather cramped – Gerald said, 'Fancy a drink?'

'That would be lovely,' replied his companion. 'I'm really enjoying myself tonight. I don't get to the theatre that often. I'm more of a cinema girl usually.'

'I know what you mean,' said Gerald, although he didn't. The last time he'd been to the cinema was probably when he was courting his wife. They'd argued about what to see so much it hardly seemed worth going again, so they hadn't.

The bar was upstairs and reaching it took some time since they were compelled to squeeze past other theatregoers on the narrow stairs. Gerald was not normally a nervous man but he wondered, not for the first time, what the chances were of a fire breaking out in this handsome old building and how on earth would everyone get out alive down the narrow corridors? The place would be in pandemonium. Best not to think about it.

Finally, they reached the bar and he told Lynn to grab a corner table while he went to get the drinks. He battled his way to the front and after a few minutes' wait, ordered two gin and tonics, then managed to carry them back to Lynn without spilling any, despite the throng of chattering theatregoers. He spotted a couple of parents from school – damn! Hopefully, they wouldn't come up and say hello, and then try to find out how their little monster was doing in class. With a bit of luck, they wouldn't notice Lynn either and put two and two together.

'This is nice isn't it, Lynn, love,' he said as he sat down and contentedly sipped his drink. 'You can't beat a bit of old-fashioned theatre.'

'Ooh yes, Gerald, you've really treated me tonight! I'm having a lovely time.' Lynn's eyes had been smiling at him but suddenly they widened and she gasped, the glass halfway to her lips. She seemed to be looking beyond Gerald's left shoulder.

'What is it?'

'Hallo Gerald.' His wife's voice had always been one that people took notice of. Now it cut through the crowd, loud and firm. People's heads turned. You could imagine it reaching the back of the lecture hall, rousing sleeping students from their doze and interrupting others who were texting and WhatsApping. 'I thought you'd be in the bar. Bet you didn't expect to see me here, did you?'

'Err…'

'There was a last minute change of plan, you see. Suzi rang and said she'd managed to get two seats for the performance. Won them in the paper, as a matter of fact, just like you did. Wasn't that funny? We were in the stalls.'

Gerald gulped. This was going to take some explaining. *Here goes*, he thought.

'Hallo love! What a nice surprise! You remember Lynn from school? I had no idea she was going to be here. We just bumped into each other, didn't we love? Graham let me down in the end, said he was double booked. Then, when I got to the theatre I spotted Lynn here on her own. Her friend couldn't make it either, could she, Lynn? Flu, didn't you say? So I said she could use my spare ticket, seeing as I had those good seats, give hers away to someone who'd turned up without, seeing as she was sitting in the gods.' He was rather pleased with himself for coming up with a plausible explanation as to why he was with Lynn.

There was a pause, during which nobody spoke. Gerald felt rather hot, his palms clammy. Finally his wife broke the silence.

'Did you now?' she said grimly, giving her husband an appraising look, before turning to Lynn with an expression of disgust on her face. 'Well, fancy that. As you've said many times, Gerald, what a remarkable coincidence.'

WONDER VISION

The press conference was going better than Mark could have dared to hope. Instead of a couple of hacks from the local rags, he had a roomful of reporters, some of them from national papers and respected websites, and a couple of bloggers too, if he wasn't mistaken. More would watch the video clip.

He resumed his pitch. 'Ladies and gentlemen, once again, thank you for coming here today. You've heard of driverless cars, right? Well, what if you were blind and you wanted to go out and about without fear? No more knocking into things, no more waiting ages for someone to help you cross the road? Sounds attractive, doesn't it? You could get your independence back, open up a whole new world of possibilities. Perhaps get a job when one was impossible before.'

'What's wrong with a guide dog?' someone shouted from the back of the room.

'OK, they're great for getting you around but they're not ideal, are they? They cost money to train for a start. Thousands of pounds. There are waiting lists. Some people have allergies. You pay a fortune in dog food.' That got a titter. 'Let's face it, they aren't for everyone. That's where my new invention comes in. Let me introduce you to Gary.'

Gary, a balding rocker wearing sunglasses with impenetrable lenses, a battered leather jacket, ripped jeans and a courier bag festooned with badges slung diagonally across his body, was helped into the room by Mark's young assistant.

'All right Gary?' The man smiled and nodded in Mark's general direction. 'Now, Gary here is blind, as you can probably tell. Notice his glasses. They are the key to my new invention. There is a wire attached to one arm of them which goes down into his bag.' Mark pointed to show the audience. 'This contains a power pack, for when he is on an extended trip, such as a day out. You could rely on hearing aid batteries if you were just popping to the shops.'

'Now, ladies and gentlemen, we're going to go outside, with Gary leading the way. He hasn't been here before, and he normally uses a white stick.'

He turned to the man. 'Feeling OK, Gary? Ready to go outside?'

Gary beamed. 'Absolutely, Mark old son. Let's do it.'

'Right, I'll just activate the glasses using this little switch on the arm. We've linked them to those speakers so everyone can hear exactly what Gary is hearing.' He pointed to two boxes, one in each corner of the stage.

Suddenly, emitting from the speakers could be heard a woman's voice. 'Turn left 90 degrees. Closed door ahead,' she said with a slight Northern twang. Gary obediently turned left and started to walk slowly towards the door. He extended both his hands and when they came into contact with the door he felt for the handle, opened it and stepped into the corridor. 'Walk straight ahead,' the woman's voice continued. 'Stop. Turn 90 degrees right. Open door.' Gary did as he was told and walked into another room. 'Stop! Obstacle immediately in front of you.' Sure enough, there was a chair blocking his path.

Mark turned to the journalists, who had been trooping behind Gary. 'I like to think of my magic glasses as a kind of satnav for blind people,' he said, 'only they are more useful as they point out obstructions. You can programme them to get you to the shops from your home, or to school, for example. Any regular route that you do frequently. Of course, you can change the voice, just like with your satnav. We do Brummie, RP, Scottish lilt, regional newsreader, you name it and we can probably get it.' *Shall I do the Glaswegian joke? Looking at this crowd, perhaps not.*

'What about Wi-Fi?' came a woman's voice. 'Do you need to have that wire trailing down all the time?'

'I'm glad you asked that. We're working on a solution,' Mark replied. 'There are a few tweaks to be made to the equipment. That's one of the reasons we need more funding.'

'Talking of funding,' said someone else, 'Where is all the money coming from for this?'

'Another good question. Crowdfunding is a marvellous thing. We've managed to solicit a significant amount of money on the funding website, but we need more if we are to hone the product until it's ready to be put on the market. Which is where you come in. If you feel you could write an article extolling the virtues of this product, we could get more publicity, attract more backers and develop the glasses until they are ready to go on sale to the general public. Which, of course, is our ultimate goal. We're not here just to make endless prototypes, we want to help the blind to see. Let's not forget that.'

Mark looked at the sea of faces. They seemed generally receptive, which was a relief. He had been nervous about this press conference, wondering if it was the right thing to do, wondering if he should have waited a bit longer, tweaked the product a little more. But it seemed to be OK. Everyone still looked interested.

'Well, if everyone has finished asking questions, then we'll wrap up—'

'I have a question.' A hand had shot up at the back.

'Yes?'

'How do we know that these so-called magic glasses are genuine?'

'Genuine? Well, I've just demonstrated them to you, with the help of Gary here. By the way, thank you very much, Gary.' There were a few claps while Gary gave a loose approximation of a wave.

'Yes, but how do we know you haven't just pre-recorded the route from one room to another, and rehearsed it with Gary?'

The audience turned to look at the source of the new voice, a black-haired man near the door. There were a couple of nods from people near him.

Mark looked surprised. 'What's your name and what publication are you from?'

'Bradley Mason from *Electrika Express.*'

'Well Bradley, I can assure you these *are* genuine, not to mention groundbreaking. Aren't you excited to be here

156

right at the start of something which could revolutionise blind people's lives? I know I am. If you want more proof, why don't you try them yourself?'

The journalist hesitated, then said, 'All right, I will.' He stepped towards Mark, who walked over to Gary and carefully unhooked the glasses from his ears. He then gave them to the man, who examined them carefully for a minute before putting them on.

'Feel free to go where you like,' Mark said, after carefully transferring the bag with protruding wires to the new speaker. 'Don't run off with them, mind! We don't want our competitors finding out all our secrets! You know what those big boys and girls are like!' Another small ripple of laughter.

The man exited the room and carried on gingerly down the corridor.

'Close your eyes for the full effect,' Mark called after him. 'The glasses will protect you!'

The woman's voice came on again. 'Door ahead.' The man opened the door and slowly stepped outside. 'Turn 45 degrees right. Walk forward. Obstruction on left. Keep walking forward. Stop! Road ahead.'

The other journalists were following the route. One of them said, 'How does she know it's a road?'

'She senses the movement and vibration of the cars, just like a blind person would, but in a safer, more consistent way,' Mark replied.

The speakers were out of earshot now but the journalist was making his way, slowly, to a pedestrian crossing. With the help, presumably, of the glasses and the beeping traffic lights, he made his way across safely, paused, then turned round and came back again when it was safe to do so, smiling broadly.

The assembled crowd clapped his efforts in between furiously tapping into phones and tablets.

He took off the glasses. 'Wow! That was quite impressive. The only thing stopping me going further was me. I'm not used to going around with my eyes shut! It was all a bit nerve-wracking. I'm sure I'd be fine when I got my confidence up.'

'Well, you're not actually blind, and that makes a lot of difference,' Mark replied. 'If you'd been blind for years, you would probably have an intuitive sense around pedestrian crossings, anyway. Remember Gary? He just needed a little practice, then he was away. Thanks for coming everyone, and if you need more details, I'll be happy to help.'

* * *

The next day, Mark reflected on the press launch. It had certainly been a success. When he'd Googled his product it had already been featured on three websites, and he'd been promised column inches in several of the newspapers and magazines that had attended. The YouTube clip he'd set up of the launch had got lots of hits already. It looked as if he was going to get his positive publicity, thank goodness. Now he could only hope that people would visit the crowdfunding site and be tempted to put money into the project. He didn't see why not –

people seemed to throw money at anything these days. You only needed a Facebook post with a sob story asking for money to go viral, and next minute you've smashed your target and made the daily news. Everyone wanted to help people who couldn't see, didn't they?

Mark liked to think of himself as an entrepreneur, a risk taker. He had taken some risks in his life, that was true. It was a far cry from his original occupation after leaving university, namely teaching English to foreigners.

After developing other products that had failed at various stages of production, his debts were mounting up alarmingly. If he could get sufficient funding for the glasses, though, he would be able to pay off those debts. Not that he'd mentioned that to the assembled journalists. Let them think the cash was solely needed to improve the launch product.

He checked his account on the crowdfunding website. Amazingly, less than 24 hours after the press launch, a not insignificant injection of cash had already been made. Fantastic! He noticed a couple of the journalists who'd attended had actually put their own money into it. There was another tranche from someone he didn't know – perhaps a contact of one of the people at the launch, who'd been passed a hot tip?

These people must have faith in me, he thought. At least somebody did. Not his own wife, that was for sure. Rebecca had given him an ultimatum at the weekend. He had a month to sort out their cash problems; otherwise, she had sworn she was going to her mother's with the kids. 'Let's hope the glasses deliver,' he muttered under his breath.

* * *

Two months later

Despite Mark's fears, Rebecca was still living in the family home. She hadn't left him. With the funds raised from his invention, he had been able to pay off nearly all his debts. Obviously, the money had been meant to go solely on the project he'd unveiled to the journalists, but he had a few, let's say, more pressing calls on the funds. Some of them – household bills – Rebecca knew about. Others – like his online gambling habit – she didn't. He hoped it would stay that way now he'd paid them off. He wouldn't let himself fall into that trap again. Well, he hoped not, anyway.

He was currently devoting all his time to working on a more advanced version of the prototype that would surely prove to be even more impressive than the initial version he'd unveiled. His mobile rang several times a day with interview requests and he'd had to hire a publicist just to cope with all the interest. The new product had been even more successful than he'd dared to hope, even though it wasn't actually in the shops.

It was a Monday. Rebecca was at the club and the kids were at school. He had just sat down to draft yet another proposal for funding when the doorbell rang.

He sighed, then got up and opened the door to find a curly-haired man in his thirties, clad in smart jeans and white shirt, open at the neck.

'Yes?'

'Mr Bannister, isn't it?' the man said, looking around Mark's hall, taking things in.

'Yes, that's right,' Mark replied uneasily. On the whole, he was suspicious of men who came to the door and said his name, unless they happened to be a courier delivering a package he'd been waiting for.

'Can I come in?'

'Err…'

'You don't remember me? Will Fisher. I was at the press launch for the glasses.'

'Oh right! Yes, now that you mention it, I do remember you. Sorry, come in.'

In fact, Mark didn't recognise the man but he was presumably another hack who had decided to bypass his publicist. A blogger who hadn't bothered to go to the launch, perhaps. Well, fine. Mark could deal with him. It was a bit inconvenient but never mind. He led him into the front living room, the one the kids were not allowed to enter. The only relatively tidy room in the house.

The man settled himself on the slouchy white leather sofa (Rebecca's choice, not his). Finding a space among the multitude of co-ordinating cushions, he looked around the room, seeming quite at home.

'I was intrigued by your new product, Mark. Very intrigued.'

'Glad to hear it. Coffee?'

'No thanks. I mean, the concept is great, isn't it? Glasses that can give blind people a whole new lease of life. And you've obtained more funding for the project, I understand?'

He must have looked up the crowdfunding website too and seen how much money we've raised so far, Mark thought. *Well, that's OK because he was probably just doing research for his article. No secrets there.*

'Yes, I'm very pleased with how it's going so far. But we need more funds before it goes into full production. It's expensive to get these things exactly right, as I'm sure you'll appreciate. What publication did you say you were from?'

'I'm freelance, as a matter of fact. Sell stories to anyone who wants them.'

'I see.'

'The thing is, Mark – may I call you that? – it's a great concept on paper but I have difficulty in accepting that the technology exists to make it a reality. There are too many variables. For one thing, surely there are too many radio waves and Wi-Fi signals bouncing around these days that would interfere with it? You know what it's like when you're driving the car with the digital radio on and it suddenly goes quiet or makes funny crackly noises when there's no reception. Surely, it wouldn't be safe to send blind people out with just a pair of glasses that could lead them straight into the traffic or smack into a wall? What if one of them had an accident? You wouldn't want bad publicity like that, would you? Or someone deciding to sue?'

Ah. A doubter. 'Well, they've managed solely with white sticks in the past. Of course, anyone using them doesn't have carte blanche to wander wherever they like.

There are still risks. They have to assess the location, decide whether they trust the glasses in a given situation, and use a bit of common sense. Perhaps they could use my invention in tandem with a stick. Or even a guide dog. But I have great faith in our technology, and surely its worth was proved during that press launch?' *If you bothered to go*, he nearly added.

Mark looked at his watch. He was getting annoyed with this stranger who had invited himself into his home. Why couldn't he just have emailed him instead of turning up on the doorstep? How did he obtain his home address, anyway? He was careful never to give that out. He had to think of Rebecca and the girls, for one thing. He would have to get rid of this man – what had he said his name was? There was definitely something about him that Mark didn't like.

The visitor had started to speak again.

'I'll get straight to the point, Mark. I think your new product is fake. You're a fraud, and I intend to go to the authorities.'

Mark didn't move. He was stunned.

'What on earth are you talking about?'

'Gary, the blind man at the press launch. Yes, I *was* there, I assure you. He's a friend of yours.'

'So what if he is? He's still blind, for God's sake.'

'You'd rehearsed his act so well, it couldn't fail. The glasses weren't talking to him, they weren't even emitting any sounds. All you'd done was prerecord some directions and play them through the speakers, making sure Gary stuck to the prepared route.'

'That's ridiculous. How can you suggest that I'd manipulate a blind man? Or are you suggesting that he's not blind? Because I can assure you, he is.'

The journalist – if that's what he was – settled back in his seat. 'Oh, I'm sure he's genuinely blind, Mark. I'm not suggesting he isn't. That would have been too risky to pull off. What if one of us had suddenly removed the glasses and realised that Gary, or whatever his name is, could actually see perfectly well? I bet he got a pay-off after we'd all gone, though. It's not ethical, Mark. You are a fraud and your product is a sham.'

Mark was trying to keep calm, not lose his temper. *Breathe*, he told himself, just like the anger counsellor had said at their last session. 'Be very careful what you accuse me of, Mr Fisher. You're forgetting that journalist who was also sceptical like you, who tried out the glasses at the press launch. You saw him. *If* you were there. How do you account for him? He became fully convinced by the glasses. As a matter of fact, he was so impressed, he's put money into the project through the crowdfunding site.'

'He was only convinced because you paid him to be. Or did you bribe him with something else?'

'What are you talking about? I don't understand.'

'There is no Bradley Mason. Or at least there are plenty of Bradley Masons on Google and Facebook, and at least one who's a journalist, so I suppose you thought you'd borrow his name in case anyone checked him out. But there's no Bradley Mason who works for *Electrika Express*. That's because it doesn't exist. I checked.'

'Of course, it exists! It's on the Internet.'

'It did until a few weeks ago. You chose a publication which actually closed last year, only they didn't take down its website until recently, so to all intents and purposes, it looked like the magazine was still going. Until you take a closer look, that is. I took a closer look, after all my emails and phone calls to them went unanswered. You should have done your research more thoroughly.'

Mark was starting to sweat now. The room had turned oppressively hot all of a sudden. What he wanted more than anything right now was a drink. That, and to get this man out of his house.

'That doesn't prove anything at all and you know it. Retract your claims or I'll set a lawyer on you.' It was all talk with this guy, wasn't it? He hoped it was.

'Mr Bannister, are you familiar with the film *The Great Escape*?'

'What has that—'

'Only there's a famous scene where the virtually blind man strides over and picks up a pin from the floor. He can't see the pin at all but he's painstakingly practised doing it, counting the exact number of paces needed, in order to deceive the others in the room into thinking his eyesight is perfect. That's what you got Bradley, or whatever his name is, to do. You coached him going outside with his eyes shut until he could do it perfectly, then made it look like the recording was directing him. Of course, in the film, the character gets found out. In Bradley's case, it worked only if he stuck exactly to the prepared route. How long did it take him to perfect it?'

'That's ridiculous! How do you account for him crossing the road safely? I could hardly have predicted the exact course of moving cars that day, could I?'

'Of course not. But you didn't have to. Bradley was simply relying on what everyone else uses – the beeper on the crossing. By that time, we couldn't hear what was coming out of the earphones and, in fact, nothing was coming out.'

'That's ridiculous!' Mark was really trying not to lose his cool. Who did this guy think he was?

'I traced "Bradley Mason" in the end. Actually, it wasn't that hard. Facebook's a wonderful tool if you're nosy, Mark, just like me. "Bradley" isn't a journalist at all and he isn't called Bradley, is he? It seems he's known you for years. Went to your wedding, that kind of thing. The perfect person to lure into your little scheme. With a significant financial inducement, I'm sure.'

Mark was having difficulty concentrating on what his uninvited guest was saying. He was aware of his own heartbeat, surely faster than usual. He was thinking, too, about Rebecca and the kids. This house. His car. How much he had to lose.

The doorbell rang again. God, who would it be this time? One of Fisher's cronies? Another hack come to expose him? He went to open the door. He was wrong. He found two young-looking policemen standing outside.

'Mr Bannister? Can we have a word, sir? Inside, if you don't mind.'

'Join the queue,' he said, sighing heavily, allowing them in but steering them into his study and away from the other visitor. 'What's all this about?' But he already knew. Knew that life was going to change for the worse, and it was all his own stupid fault.

Suddenly, his clever scheme to make money didn't seem so clever, after all. He'd only done it to pay off his debts, keep Rebecca from running off back to her parents, taking the kids with her. He'd thought it would solve everything. Thought he was being so clever. Well, it had been Gillespie who'd actually suggested the concept of the glasses, one night in the pub when they'd had a few drinks, just the three of them. Funny how the best ideas always seemed to start off in the pub. Only now it was looking like the worst idea in the world. It had begun almost as a bet really, but having come up with a model, Mark had gone on and started to develop a prototype. His shortlived career in design and technology had come in useful, after all.

He had realised that there was money to be made from launching a product that would raise the hopes of blind people. He knew the scheme had the potential to raise lots of cash from trusting investors. And at that point in his life, it was cash that he needed. Badly needed. Rebecca was getting fed up of all his projects, which started off so well but came to nothing, always involving significant quantities of money which he would go on to lose. The sure-fire schemes that, sooner or later, always failed.

To begin with, just after they'd married, she'd helped him out with her own money, even got her parents to invest on one occasion. But that soon stopped when they realised they would never get a return, so he'd been forced to find other ways to raise cash. Hence, the online gambling – what *had* he been thinking? And remortgaging the house, which he'd had to keep from Rebecca, in case she started asking too many questions. The strain of it all… it was too much.

The young policeman was speaking again, while the other one, expressionless, stood looking at Mark, notebook in hand. Did they still use notebooks?

'We've received a complaint, sir, about you attempting to defraud members of the public. A serious offence, as I'm sure you'll agree. Shall we sit down?'

PRETTY ORDINARY

I'm just an ordinary guy, really. Like everyone else in nearly all respects. I mean, if you happened to be passing me in the street, you definitely wouldn't look twice at me. I have no illusions about that. Just your average bloke, average height – maybe a little shorter, if I'm being really honest. Receding hairline, even though I won't admit it to anyone. A few grey hairs, even, around the temples. Must do something about that. Anyway, I like being able to walk down the street without getting recognised; not having to wear sunglasses in the depths of winter and a big baseball cap like some of those celebs you see in the magazines. Being in the limelight, it's not for everyone, is it?

My childhood was not so ordinary, I suppose, although it seemed ordinary to me at the time. We travelled a lot. My dad worked in embassies. Not an ambassador or anything as grand as that – he was one of the support staff behind the scenes. I'm a bit hazy as to what he actually did, but I remember that he'd always been good at languages. He read Arabic at university, but he could pick up pretty much any tongue if he put his mind to it. Unlike me – I'm a rubbish linguist.

When I was a boy, we lived in Africa for a good few years – Malawi, Kenya and Rhodesia, before finishing up in South Africa, Dad's longest posting. We had a comfortable expat life, for the most part, mixing with the other Westerners – I didn't realise how privileged we were compared with the local people of the countries we were living in. Looking back now, I can see it all right, see the injustice of it all, but as a child, it felt perfectly normal to have full-time maids, housekeepers and gardeners. Perfectly normal for them to use a different entrance from us when entering our house. Perfectly OK to make sure that they drank out of different cups from us white people. Growing up, I never gave it a thought.

Anyway, apart from a decent house, Dad's job gave him all sorts of perks, including free flights back to the UK for all of us – Mum, me and my younger brother Nat. We did come back once a year to stay with my grandparents, who had a rambling house in the Surrey Hills. But we mostly stayed overseas, wherever my father had been posted. He could have sent me and my brother to an English boarding school if he'd wanted – the government would have paid – but he chose to send us to international schools instead, in whichever country we happened to be living in. So every couple of years, my brother and I got to change school. It sounds terrible but, in fact, we quite liked it.

Nearly all the children were in the same boat, for a start, and you learned to make friendships easily with the other Western kids in the school. There were French, German, Italian and Spanish pupils, but English was the preferred means of communication, luckily for me. (There *were* American kids but they tended to go to their own schools.) I suppose if I'd stayed longer in a school, they might have picked up on the fact that I'm different from other people in one way. But nobody did. The teachers were too busy trying to get everyone up to the same level, constantly having to accommodate new arrivals who'd only set foot in the country the previous week. With so many of the children not having English as their first language, it was easy for the less able kids to pass through school without anybody noticing they needed extra help.

The teachers had enough to deal with, anyway. They had to battle with the realities of African life, anything from frequent power cuts to water shortages to floods.

I was of average intelligence, I suppose, able to keep up with the curriculum (at least at first), which was traditional in those days and had lots of aspects of the English public school system. Also, I tended not to do things that were likely to attract attention, which definitely helped me to blend in more.

Unlike my brother. When we were living in Nairobi, I remember the time he found a scorpion in the dust just outside the school grounds. Instead of running away – which is what I would have done – or alerting one of the staff, he somehow managed to manoeuvre it into a large matchbox with the aid of a couple of sticks and brought it into the dinner hall, whereupon he released it on the floor, sending some of the girls, and a few of the boys, up on chairs and into a shrieking panic.

Hughie, a freckled schoolboy from Hampshire, whose father was something important in the High Commission, was the bravest boy in the school. He crushed the thing with his foot, leaving the cooks to brush up the pieces before they could serve us our traditional English lunch – probably shepherd's pie and bread and butter pudding or something stodgy like that.

For that misdemeanour, Nat received a Saturday morning detention. He took this particularly hard as we were allowed to visit the busy local market on Saturdays and would spend all our pocket money on garishly coloured sweets, most of which would be eaten before we got back home. I, on the other hand, had the distinction of being the only boy in my class *not* to receive a detention that year. This I put down more to luck than being a goody-goody.

Nat is now an accountant in Buckinghamshire, married with two kids. Not the kind of life I'd want, but he seems content enough. Enough of him though. This story is about me, not my brother. Let's go back to the beginning.

I always think I was born with two disadvantages. I say born, but one of those disadvantages was given to me five days after I came into the world. Since you ask, it's my first name. I don't really want to reveal it to you, but I suppose there's no harm in it. It's Larkin. I mean, what kind of a name is that? To me, it sounds like some sort of Medieval ball game, but probably what pops into your head, if you've reached a certain age, is the poet Philip Larkin.

Of course, I was teased in the playground. 'Posh is she, your mum?' 'Larkin' about' became my default nickname and every time I changed teachers, on first meeting me they would always say something like, 'Larkin? Oh, that's unusual. After the poet, is it?'

After at least three teachers had come out with the same line, I wanted to scream, '*No! It's not after the poet! My mum's never read a scrap of poetry in her life!*' but I'd usually mumble 'Yes, that's right sir,' for a quiet life. And as it turned out, while I was rubbish at foreign languages, English was my best subject at school.

When she was still alive, my mother said she'd given my name to me because the day I was born, two weeks early, Dad wanted to name me Geoff after the footballer he idolised at the time. She couldn't stand that name because she'd heard it so often at school (before she'd married, mum had been a dinner lady in the Midlands for years) so she had to come up with something at short notice, and wanted something a bit unusual, a moniker that would stand out.

Short notice? Why on earth hadn't she been thinking of names for nearly nine months? I mean, I may have been unexpected but once she knew I was on the way, surely it was 50:50 that she'd need a boy's name. Seems they were both so convinced I was going to be a girl, they didn't bother with boys' names until I actually popped out.

I've changed it now. My name, I mean. It's easy enough to do these days. When I first left school I used to use Larkin as my surname, but I still didn't like it. So I went for something completely different, more in keeping with what I'm doing now. If I told you, you might have heard of it.

Anyway, it was when I was around seven years old that I first realised I had another disadvantage, one which I had presumably been born with – a disability, if you can call it that. Not a major one, you understand, but enough to affect the course of my whole life. When I was in lessons, I would often not catch what the teacher was saying. In music classes, it seemed as if they were only playing half the notes of a tune. In school assembly, I couldn't follow the words properly.

It took me quite a while to realise that I wasn't hearing exactly what everyone else was hearing. It definitely affected my schoolwork because I was falling behind by secondary school. What teachers said in front of the blackboard just wasn't making sense. I know why now.

Bizarrely, I found I could have a normal conversation with anyone, even if they had their back to me, as long as they were speaking calmly and on one level. But most people vary their tone of voice and don't even realise they are doing it. When I was 14, my mother took me to the doctor to have my hearing tested, only to have him say, 'There's nothing wrong with that boy, Mrs Smythson. It's just inattention. Make sure he sits at the front of the class.'

Well, that didn't work, so one holiday they took me to a specialist on London's Harley Street, after much grumbling from my father about the cost. After shining a light down my ear, plonking some headphones on me and subjecting me to various weird sounds, he gave his verdict.

They say that cats are capable of hearing sounds at ultra-high frequencies, unlike humans. I read in the newspaper that if you jingle coins or rub foil sheets together, it can cause a seizure in some cats because of the sounds produced, which only they can hear. Poor cats, is all I can say. Their worlds must be a lot noisier than ours. I used to have a cat and I swear she didn't like it when I pressed the buttons on the remote control to change TV channels, even though I couldn't hear a thing.

With me though, it's the opposite phenomenon from the sounds that a cat hears. I'm not deaf but I hear an incredibly restricted range of frequencies. It's not just the extremes at either end of the sound chart either, which is common enough, especially as you get older. I couldn't care less if I can't hear very high frequencies. Who wants to be like a bat? What *does* matter is that I can't hear the nuances of speech even in a normal conversation, and might well miss out on vital details if the person's voice is pitched too high or too low. Listening to some men – and women – with deep voices, it's a nightmare because I hardly hear anything of what they say. The same goes for anyone with a high-pitched voice or excitable children. Perhaps that's why I never married.

I don't tell people, because in the past, when I said that I had trouble catching words, their immediate reaction was to speak slowly and loudly – or shout, even – not realising that this doesn't work at all. I've become quite practised at lipreading, it has to be said. It's definitely not the same as conventional deafness and I thought no one else would have the same condition as me, but there's a man in San Francisco who also suffers from it, apparently. That's what my consultant said, anyway. I've Googled it but there's really not much information at all out there. My condition is so rare it doesn't even have a name.

In everyday life, I can disguise it fairly successfully. It's amazing what you can get done these days just by tapping a few buttons on your phone, without having to actually speak to someone. When email came in, it was a blessing for me; likewise, texting and any other messaging involving a keyboard.

It's true that I left school with a clutch of rather mediocre exam passes, much to my parents' dismay, and drifted into various jobs, unlike my brother, who was focused on starting a career. I worked in a shop at one point, when I needed the money, and it was all right when people were simply paying for their purchases but if they asked questions or had a complaint, it was a nightmare. I simply couldn't make out a lot of what they were saying.

Still, a regular job wouldn't have suited me anyway – never mind my hearing. I've never really been one for nine to five, which is just as well given the profession I've ended up in.

You see, although I don't get much out of listening to the radio and I may not be able to hear all the notes in a tune, when it comes to live music, it's a different matter entirely. As a teenager, I went to a few concerts and was amazed how I could sort of absorb the music in a way that I never had with recordings. It was as if I could sense the notes that would normally have been much too high for me to make out. I found out that I have an excellent sense of rhythm, too. I feel the vibrations through my fingers and translate them into drumstick beats. It's easy once you know how. I can cope with even the most complex rhythms, stuff that other people would take years to master.

That's what led to my current employment, if you can call it that. I'm known as one of the masters of my art – imagine that! People come from miles away – other countries, even from the other side of the world – just to hear me do my stuff. I've had columns and columns written about me in the press and there are several websites set up by my fans, devoted to me and my musical output. Amazing, really, when you think about it.

I do worry, though. It's given me more than a few sleepless nights over the years, I can tell you. What if someone should find out? I mean, when I first joined the band, I made some remark about being a bit deaf and all the others laughed and said, 'Everyone's a bit deaf here mate, we only play at one volume and it's extra loud.' Tinnitus comes with the job, doesn't it?

Now it's five years down the line and we're famous, with three number 1 albums and several awards, I keep thinking I'll be rumbled by the press. A top musician who can't hear music? Who is, effectively, tone deaf? How ridiculous is that? Imagine the headlines. When the band sings live onstage, it looks like I'm singing too but, actually, I'm just forming the words with my mouth without making a noise because, otherwise, how could I sing the high and low notes in tune? The song would be ruined. The band members know I don't sing (although they don't know the real reason) and, thankfully, they're cool about it – they need my drumming skills too much to complain.

I won't tell you what name I use now that Larkin's dead and buried because that would make it easy to find out the name of the band. You see, I don't want anyone giving away my secret, not now we're so successful. You can Google all you like but I've been careful not to tell anyone, not to reveal anything in interviews.

Growing up, I had no idea my life would turn out like this. I suppose the travelling has parallels, although we don't visit Africa too often. We're almost constantly on the road with the band – we only got back from our US tour last week, which lasted a massive eight months. Then, in a few days, we're off to Asia, which has our biggest fanbase and, consequently, makes us the most money. It's tiring all right, but the financial rewards make it well worthwhile. Oh, yes. I own three properties now and a couple of rather flash cars, not to mention various investments that my accountant said were a good idea. Who'd have thought we'd be playing places like Madison Square Gardens and the O2 Arena? Not me, that's for sure. Yet if I wear ordinary clothes, I can still get away with popping to the shops without being bothered. No one notices the drummer…

These days I have too much at stake for anyone to find out my secret. I've got used to the life, you see. My parents died a few years ago and as far as I know, they never told anyone about my condition. No one ever told my brother, certainly, and I haven't properly been in touch with him since the band became famous. Since we left school, we've never been close and now we're just down to exchanging Christmas cards, nothing more. And I get my PA to send those. In fact, nobody knows except my consultant, and I've always thought he's more of a classical music lover. Opera, not O2.

So, I'll leave it there, if you don't mind. Mustn't be late for rehearsals.

REVENGE

'I've got just the one for you, Mr Hardy,' said the grey-haired, stocky woman wearing a battered old Barbour jacket and slacks of an indeterminate colour with, if he wasn't mistaken, more than a scattering of fur on them. She had run the animal sanctuary near Tom's home for decades. In fact, he could remember visiting it as a young boy with his mother and sister. It must have made a big impression on him. He recalled rows and rows of wooden pens, each containing a dog or a cat, or sometimes even a rabbit. There didn't seem to be anything else in the pens – just a bit of straw, perhaps.

Nowadays, there were smaller animals like hamsters and guinea pigs and they had fancy gyms made out of cardboard boxes and loo roll, and the larger ones had comfy looking beds and lots of toys. The strong animal smell he remembered from his youth was still there, pervading the place, and so was the constant noise of dogs yapping or whining. It was obviously run on a shoestring.

There had been a rusty collecting tin, he remembered, near the way out, and at the end of their visit, his mother had given him a few pennies to put in the slot. He'd asked if they could take one of the animals home but she had said, 'Not today, Tom. I've got my hands full with you and Nancy and the menagerie we already have. We only came for a look round before tea. Maybe next time.'

Only came for a look round. Why did I come here, of all places, today? thought Tom to himself, casting his eye around the old place once more.

The woman was pointing to the pen in the corner. 'He's in this one here. What do you think? Isn't he a beauty?'

Tom peered in through the cage. He was certainly striking. Big – well, huge would be a better word, with puffed up cheeks and long whiskers – and entirely grey except for a tiny patch of white on the tip of his immensely thick, fluffy tail.

According to the little handwritten plaque, taped wonkily to the cage, his name was Monty. A fine name, thought Tom, for a fine specimen. Nothing embarrassing about that. Not like his sister's rescue dog, Budgie. What a ridiculous name for a dog! And a bull mastiff at that. She must feel ridiculous when calling him in the park. No doubt, it was an 'ironic' name chosen by his brother in law.

Tom poked a finger experimentally through the bars, only to withdraw it hastily a second later as Monty lunged towards him, baring his teeth and claws. Celia – yes, that was her name, he remembered now – started to laugh. 'He's a bit of a handful, that one,' she said. 'I'm sure you'll cope though, Mr Hardy. He's made for you, don't you think?'

Tom considered. Why he'd decided to visit the rescue centre, he couldn't say. Tuesday was normally his day to visit the library, after popping out for the paper. He wasn't sure what had made him turn the corner and keep walking until he'd reached the edge of the village, where a gate marked the entrance to the sanctuary. Still, now he was here…

The boy *was* handsome. Feisty too, by the looks of it, but Tom could cope with that. It was only a pet, after all. Growing up in the countryside, he'd had all sorts of pets as a boy – starting with a rat, then progressing to ferrets and even a chicken (until he forgot to close her coop properly one night, and the next morning all that was left was a pile of feathers).

He loved animals but his wife had been allergic to them. She couldn't be in the same room as a dog or a cat without coming out in a coughing fit. It was a shame really, especially as they'd never had children. He would have loved to have more pets.

This was a magnificent beast, though. He could imagine Monty stretched out contentedly on his master's lap while Tom rubbed his silky ears. After Trina's death, he needed a companion. Everyone said so and after a year (it was the anniversary of her death, in fact, this very day), Tom had conceded that they could just be right. It would be nice to have someone else living with him in the old house again. Someone to talk to, even if they couldn't exactly talk back.

He looked at Monty, who was busily engaged in scratching his ear. How much of a handful could he be?

'I'll take him.'

So, after filling in a form and handing over a generous donation (Celia didn't seem to be worried about doing a home visit to check it was suitable), Monty came to live in the house on the corner of Elvedon Lane with Tom.

They got into a comfortable routine, just the two of them. Tom was delighted to have a companion, who was (usually) pleased to see him and happy to be stroked (what lustrous, soft fur!) and who obligingly followed him about the house, calmly sitting and watching him do the ironing, or begging for scraps while Tom ate his dinner. When he was reading the paper, he would hear Monty's wheezy snores as he curled up on the sofa next to his master. Sometimes, Monty would bat the paper away when he wanted exclusive use of Tom's lap, circling around twice before settling down contentedly.

When he was upstairs on the computer, Monty would silently pad underneath his desk and stay there until Tom had finished. Unless it was dinnertime, in which case Monty would leap up onto the keypad and generally make a nuisance of himself until Tom got up and fed him. And when Tom went out, he would often see Monty's face at the living room window when he returned, as if to welcome him back. If he'd been gone a long time, though, Monty would turn his back on Tom in a huff, only deigning to turn round when he heard the unmistakable rattle of the treat tin.

* * *

Then, four years after Monty arrived, things changed in Elvedon Lane. One day, Tom was making his daily trip into the back garden to feed crumbs to the birds.

The ground had iced up overnight and he slipped on the outside steps. Cursing, Tom couldn't help but fall awkwardly and winded himself. It was some time before he managed to drag himself into the kitchen, watched silently by Monty, and locate his mobile to ring for help. After a marathon wait on a trolley in A&E, a broken hip was diagnosed and Tom was told that he would have to have an operation to replace it if he wanted to walk properly again.

He waited months for the operation, then, despite the surgeon's optimism, it was not a great success. Complications set in and although Tom recovered to some extent, life became much more difficult for him. He had trouble moving around now, even with a stick, and hardly left the house.

'It's old age, Monty,' he said one day. 'Comes to us all. Even you, I expect.' Monty regarded him through narrowed eyes before trotting, tail bolt upright, to his empty food bowl. 'All right, all right, I know what you want,' chuckled Tom as he shuffled over to the larder in search of a tin.

As time went on, Tom found it more difficult to manage without help. He thought he was going to have to give up the house he loved, which was still full of memories of Trina. He dreaded the day, because he knew he would have to give up Monty. They never allowed pets in sheltered housing, did they? Tom didn't know if he could stand that. To lose Trina, then Monty too?

So he put off doing anything about it for as long as he could. Then, after he'd finally made enquiries, the woman from the council rang back at last. She said the agency they used had found a part-time carer, and did Tom want to meet him?

The next day, the doorbell rang. Tom opened the door to find a tall young man with short spiky hair, ripped jeans and one diamond stud in his ear, who introduced himself as 'Karl from the agency'. His new carer. Tom wasn't too impressed but as he reminded himself, he didn't have much choice. It was this or end his days in a nursing home smelling of piss, sitting comatose in a high-backed chair with all the other residents, in front of mindless programmes on daytime television. Just the thought made him shudder.

His new carer spotted the grey shadow slinking behind Tom's legs, tail twitching.

'Was that a cat? Only I don't do cats normally. Didn't they tell you?'

'No,' replied Tom. 'They didn't.'

So he made another phone call to the agency, but it seemed that Karl was the only carer available, and what's more, Tom was very lucky to have him. 'Some of the people on our list have been waiting for months,' the woman on the phone told him briskly. 'It's that or go to the other agency, and heaven knows what they charge. The stories you hear about them…' She trailed off delicately. Tom hadn't heard any stories, but given the tone of the woman's voice, it seemed decidedly unwise to try them out.

* * *

'I'm coming in for now,' Karl said on his first day, 'but I've told them it's not long term. On account of my asthma.'

'Err… right,' said Tom, exchanging a look with Monty, who was wearing what could be called a somewhat disdainful expression. Sometimes, that cat seemed almost human.

Karl's duties were to help Tom get dressed and down to breakfast, and then prepare his meals in advance, for Tom to heat up later in the microwave. In the evenings, he would assist Tom to get up the stairs, and help him get ready for bed (as well as, reluctantly, put down a bowl for Monty. Tom found it difficult to bend these days). All this had to be done in 30 minutes flat, twice a day, and Karl was always rushing so as to get to his next client. It seemed to take him as long to write up his daily notes in the ring binder as it did for him to actually do any 'caring'.

Having been on his own for so long (excepting Monty, of course), Tom found another presence in the house difficult to get used to at first. The only person who saw him on a regular basis now (well, aside from the postman, the milkman and the cleaner) was his younger sister, Nancy, who lived about twenty miles away, but she was getting on in years herself.

It was the disruption of their routine that Tom (and Monty) could have done without. Karl would put things back in the wrong place – tea towels, mugs, the packet of sugar – and the other day he had even found the time to clear out Tom's fridge when there was perfectly good food inside that Tom just hadn't quite got round to eating before the use-by date. So the smelly hunk of Stilton that Tom had been saving for that day's lunch had been thrown out, as had the week-old carton of custard that would have been perfectly all right to have with his apple pie that evening.

Tom's newspaper would mysteriously disappear before he'd had time to read the article on page 7 that he was saving for later. 'Oh, I put them all in recycling if you want to have a rummage,' Karl would say casually, knowing perfectly well that Tom couldn't get to the recycling box, as it was past the back garden steps where Tom never ventured since he'd had his tumble.

Monty didn't seem to be a fan of Karl either. He never went near him, for one thing, ever since the carer had forgotten to feed him one night when Tom was ill in bed. As with many cats, the way to Monty's heart was through his stomach.

Mind you, Monty and Nancy didn't have a great relationship, either. One day, Nancy had come to visit and, without thinking, left her powder blue cashmere cardigan draped on the sofa. Barely a minute later, Monty had leapt up onto the sofa, carefully padded onto the cardigan, circled around a few times to make his new bed a bit comfier, then lay down on it, depositing a fine coating of grey hairs for good measure. Nancy was furious and when she tried to drag him off, he had dug his claws in indignantly and let out a furious meow, even hissing at her. 'Bad cat!' she shouted as Monty eventually jumped off in disgust, but Tom secretly thought it rather funny. It seemed that Monty, now glaring at Tom's sister from the furthest corner of the room, only had eyes for his master.

* * *

On that particular Thursday, when it happened, it was a rainy, windy winter's day just before Christmas. The daylight had already started to fade by three o'clock and by the time Karl, who was early, rang the doorbell to announce his presence, it was pitch black. He let himself in with the key Tom had given him. In any case, Tom was engrossed in watching the climax of an old war film on television.

'Afternoon, Mr Hardy! Everything all right?' called Karl loudly, then marched through to the kitchen without waiting for a reply. Suddenly, there was a loud, 'Waaaaaaaaaa!' followed by Karl shouting 'Blasted cat! Get out of the way!' Unseen by Tom, who was still watching the movie, Karl aimed a kick at Monty, who dodged past and sped out through the cat flap.

'That's it! No food for you, stupid animal. Hunt for it yourself. That'll teach you to get in my way. Should never have come to a house with a cat.' Muttering and sniffing to himself, Karl went about the rest of his jobs at breakneck speed, as usual.

By the time he'd prepared supper and got Tom ready for bed, it was only five o'clock. But paid carers – especially Karl, who had a job on the side as an escort for lonely professional forty-somethings that he hadn't told the agency about – are always hurrying to get somewhere else. Why should they give a fig if it's only the middle of the afternoon when they are putting a grown man to bed in his pyjamas? 'All set, Mr Hardy? Right, I'll see you tomorrow then. Ta-ra,' said Karl as he bustled out of the bedroom, feeling in his back pocket for his timesheet. *Thank God it's nearly Friday*, he was thinking. *One more day, then I can forget about all these geriatric time-wasters 'til Monday.* He was thinking of giving in his notice anyway. Being an escort was much more lucrative, not to mention more fun. Not many jobs gave you the chance to go to restaurants, films and exhibition first nights *and* get paid for it.

Now it was at this moment that the ancient lamp on the table on the landing, given to them as a wedding present by Trina's uncle, chose to wobble (probably on account of it being placed too near to the edge by the cleaner on her last visit), causing the heavy ceramic base to topple over the edge of the table and smash to the floor. The bulb broke and Karl was plunged into darkness. He had to feel his way to the unlit stairs, as the downstairs hall light was off too because it needed a new bulb. (Tom was far too tottery now to go up a ladder to replace it and when he'd asked Karl to help, the carer had declared that it wasn't in his job description to be a maintenance person.)

What happened next could later only be guessed at. From his bedroom, Tom heard a thump but as he was now listening to a programme on Radio Four and the discussion was getting rather interesting, he didn't think to investigate. When the broadcast was over, he switched off his own lamp, rolled over and went to sleep as normal. He'd always been quite a heavy sleeper.

The next day, Friday, Karl didn't turn up to get Tom out of bed. Tom waited for an hour, then two, and then three because he didn't want to make a fuss. Finally, his bladder couldn't wait any longer, so he was forced to haul himself out of bed and into the bathroom, which took some time. He was never good in the mornings. He dressed himself with difficulty and it was only as he was preparing to go downstairs that he caught sight of something that he definitely hadn't been expecting.

There, sprawled face down at the bottom of the stairs, was Karl in his green carer's uniform. What on earth had happened? There was something odd about him (well, apart from being spread-eagled on the tiles) and it took Tom a few seconds to realise that his head was positioned at a strange angle.

Just then, Monty strolled into the hall and silently regarded the lifeless body, before sitting down next to it and calmly starting to wash his face with his front paw. It was the closest Tom had ever seen Monty get to Karl.

'Monty,' said Tom, 'I think I'd better ring 999.'

* * *

A week later, Nancy, fully coordinated as usual, and with her hair freshly seen to by the hairdresser, was round on her regular monthly visit. Tom was making do with tinned soup and sandwiches until the agency could supply him with a new carer. Nancy perched on the edge of the sofa drinking a cup of tea while looking around the room suspiciously, on the eye out for dust.

'I told you that cat was evil.'

'Don't be ridiculous, Nan, you can't blame a pet. Are you telling me he did it on purpose? That's the most outlandish thing I've ever heard. Apart from anything else, cats aren't that bright. Have you seen the size of a cat's brain compared with a dog's? I did once, in a museum. It was tiny. All Monty is interested in is his food and his milk.'

'Well, it seems strange if you ask me. That carer must have tripped over something on those stairs when the lights were off. That lamp that smashed was too far away. Nobody had moved anything. The police said he had grey fur on his trouser legs. You told me Monty never went near him normally. Grey cat in the dark…'

'I didn't ask you. Stairs can be tricky, especially when you can't see anything. He was probably hurrying. Always in a hurry, he was. We've all slipped on the stairs at least once. It was just unlucky.' He paused. 'Well, more than unlucky. Then, when he was on the floor, Monty probably used him as a seat or something. It's what cats do. But you wouldn't know that seeing as you don't have one. Anyway, you can't stand cats, especially after Monty ruined your cardigan. You'd blame anything on him, given half a chance.'

'Well, it might interest you to know that I bumped into Celia today. You know, from the sanctuary. She was in the big Sainsbury's, picking up the tins people had donated for the animals. I told her what they think happened last week.'

'Nan, I don't want you broadcasting…'

'The thing is, she told me something interesting. Very interesting. You weren't the first person to adopt Monty, you know.'

'What are you getting at? Of course, I wasn't his first owner. I know that. Why do you think he was in the sanctuary in the first place?'

'Well, there were *two* lots before you, according to Celia. The first family gave him away. Never said why, apparently. Celia reckons they had a baby and didn't want to risk that huge monster with it. The claws. Toxoplasmosis. You know.'

'Plenty of people manage babies *and* cats, Nan—'

'Anyway, they gave him to the sanctuary and Celia says she'd barely got him settled in his new cage when this elderly lady came for a tour and fell in love with him. Well, he's unusual, I'll give you that. Not your usual tabby. This woman – Gwendoline, her name was. Lovely name. You don't hear it now. She lived by herself in the village. Never married.

'Well, she'd had him for a few weeks and everything seemed fine, then one day she forgot to feed him. The cat bowl, tin opener, tin of cat food… they found them all out ready on the worktop. She'd just forgotten, they reckoned. Maybe she was developing dementia. Who knows?'

'I don't see the relevance of— '

'Let me finish. You always were too impatient. Well, her neighbour was due to give her a lift to the bingo but no one came to the door when she rang. So this neighbour let herself in with a key and found Gwendoline unconscious in the hall. She'd hit her head on the hall table. Antique it was. Must have tripped over something, but there was nothing there; except for a hungry cat who tried to claw the neighbour in its eagerness for supper. They rushed Gwendoline to hospital but she never recovered.'

'But you don't really think that he... are you saying that Monty deliberately made her trip up, just because she allegedly forgot to feed him? And that, years later, he's the cause of Karl's death too? You're mad, Nan. I always said that satellite TV you watch is a menace.'

'All I'm saying, Tom, is it's a bit of a coincidence, isn't it? You said yourself you've nearly tripped over him a couple of times. It's easily done.'

'But he doesn't get in the way on purpose, Nan! He's just a cat, and he gets hungry. And he's staying with me,' Tom added in a determined voice.

Just then came the familiar thwack of the cat flap swinging open. Seconds later, Monty appeared from the kitchen, sleek and silent. He stood stock still for a minute, glanced over at Tom, then regarded Nancy for several seconds with his huge amber eyes, the only movement being the rapid swish of his magnificent tail. Then he padded out again, leaping through the flap into the garden. Tom busied himself with making another cup of tea for his sister. A few minutes later, they heard the swing of the cat flap again. Then, there he was, by the kitchen door. Without making a sound, he stalked over to Nancy. Before she could stop him, he crouched on his haunches and suddenly leapt up onto her lap, while at the same time, delicately depositing something on to it that had been in his jaws. Something greyish brown. Something with a long tail. Something that was still wriggling.

The screams could be heard all the way down the street.

THE CROSSING

Local news report

Coastguards today scaled back their search for a man believed to have been swept off the deck of the Seacross ferry while on its way from Rosslare to Holyhead. It is now two days since Conor O'Riordan, 42, a teacher from County Wicklow, was last seen on the vessel and hopes have faded of finding him alive.

* * *

He had never wanted to go to England. Not then. It was too soon. But Mairead had insisted, telling him that he was boring for wanting to stay in his hometown. 'It's only England for God's sake, not feckin' Mongolia. I haven't seen Fergus for years. Not since that Christmas when he came back to Dublin for a couple of days. So we're going. The ferry's booked, so it is.'

Conor gazed out of the window of their small flat. Was this what he wanted? To be bossed around by a woman nearly ten years younger than him? At the start of their relationship perhaps he would have said yes, that was exactly what he wanted. Back then Conor O'Riordan, 40, had been still living in his county of birth, with a decent job as a teacher in a secondary school, it was true, but still single and still feeling there was something missing in his life. Companionship, kindred spirits, love – call it what you will.

Then along came Mairead with her sparkling green eyes, pale, freckly skin and long, thick auburn hair with just the hint of a curl that reached below her shoulders. She was training to be a teacher and on secondment in his school, just for a term.

Nothing happened between them while she was working at St Mark's College. Conor was much too shy, for a start, and besides, Francis O'Malley from the French department had got in before him, inviting Mairead out for a drink when she'd hardly finished her first week. For most of that term, Conor had barely talked to the new trainee, beyond a mumbled 'sorry' when he accidentally bumped into her one day in the staff room.

Francis O'Malley got nowhere with her, which surprised none of his colleagues. His record with the trainees was not good. The longest relationship he'd had, with Ciara who hadn't even lasted a term at the school, was over after five weeks. No one knew what had happened and Francis himself was cagey about it, but there was plenty of speculation among Conor and his fellow teachers as to what had gone wrong.

Looking back at that term, Conor could see how he'd missed the signs that Mairead was interested in him. She would volunteer to do extra work in his English class, for a start, helping some of the weaker pupils, although he always turned her down out of embarrassment. He didn't want it to seem as if he couldn't cope with the class, even if at times it felt exactly like that. He'd been teaching nearly the whole time after leaving college, after all, except for that brief stint working in the local library. He'd thought the quiet would suit him but actually he was just bored, and anyway, as the most junior there, the job seemed to mostly involve telling schoolchildren to stop eating and throwing out homeless people at the end of the day. His move to teaching wasn't exactly a vocation – more to do with the fact that he couldn't think what else he wanted to do.

He did have a proper conversation with Mairead at the staff Christmas party, when they ended up discussing their favourite books. Conor was a voracious reader and could have chatted about different titles for hours. It was a stroke of genius (or more probably luck) that caused Mairead to bring up the one subject that he could talk confidently about.

That was it, though, until Conor had a friend request from her on his Facebook account, after she'd left. Normally, he barely looked at the site. It was too depressing finding out the exciting things his old school friends were doing, how they'd married and produced four kids all of a sudden, or been promoted or emigrated or something. In the event, he found himself keeping in touch with her online for all of the spring term, when she had moved into another school a few miles away.

It was Mairead who had first asked if he wanted to sup a pint of Guinness in her local pub. He'd half thought she'd chosen the place so she could invite her friends round to laugh at him, such was his self-confidence in those days. But to his great surprise, the evening went well. They found they had more in common than a love of books – both of them loved walking, hated sport and were more than ready to escape the clutches of their respective families. Mairead, he learnt, was the eldest of five and sick of being called on to babysit her younger brothers. The more she chatted about her life, the more he liked her.

In fact, the evening went so well that Conor found he could summon up the courage to invite her out to the cinema to see the current blockbuster. This was followed by hiking in the Wicklow Mountains and even a shopping trip to Dublin, where Mairead insisted on picking out some new clothes for him.

'I'm just sayin', Conor, you need some new stuff. You can't be wearin' band T-shirts for the rest of your life, for the love of God.' It was nice to be taken care of for a change, and before he knew it, they had become a couple. 'I'm too old for you,' he'd protest, a tiny part of him hoping she'd agree, so he could go back to his old, comfortable ways, the life she'd known nothing about. The life no one knew about, not even those closest to him. 'I told you, I like older men,' she'd retort, squeezing his hand and smiling that wide, freckly smile of hers that he just couldn't resist.

Well, maybe this was the way my life was meant to turn out, he remembered thinking when they were a few months into their relationship. *Maybe I was wrong.*

* * *

Two and a half years later, and they were still together, still going out to the cinema, shopping in Dublin at weekends, and having nice meals in fancy restaurants when they could afford it, fish and chips from the chippie down the road when they couldn't. He had met all her friends – she had a lot – and she had met his, who could almost be counted on one hand – just the few he had kept from school, and one or two of his teaching colleagues.

It felt comfortable. Safe. Undemanding. Except that he was sick of it. Sick of avoiding the big question, fielding jokes from his friends, skirting around the inevitable issue of *When Are Youse Two Going To Get Engaged?* which had now assumed scary capital letters in his mind.

His oldest and closest friend Brendan was forever making jokes about 'the longest pre-engagement this century' and saying, 'Watch out, first she'll want a puppy and then it'll be a baby. Seriously though Con, when are you gonna propose? Sean got hitched ages ago and it's about time we had another party.'

In truth, Conor wanted to get out of the whole thing but he was too far in, had spent too many Sunday lunches with Mairead's parents in Kilkenny to back out now, met too many of her friends, seen too many knowing looks passing between them. There was his mother to think of, too, now that Da had passed away.

Years ago, his younger sister Niamh had, aged 22, married Seamus, settled down and had three kids in quick succession, to the delight of their mother, with another one on the way by the look of it (surely, a mistake? She was 38 now, after all). She seemed happy enough but always looked so tired, with dark circles around her eyes. Seamus was a nice enough bloke but when he and the clan came round for Sunday lunch at Conor and Niamh's mother's house, Conor noticed that he never seemed to smile anymore. They had given up holidays. Most of their money went on the kids, from what Conor could make out – clothes and shoes and expensive after-school activities and holiday clubs.

Is that what I want? Really? To be chained to the same woman for the rest of my life? No freedom to be myself? Loads of kids when I get enough of them at school as it is?

Conor already knew the answer.

I'll just do this one trip to keep her happy, let her see her brother, and then I'll tell her, he thought as he loaded up the car with Mairead's trio of hefty bags and his own small rucksack. End it. He might have to move away from here – go west to Cork perhaps, or up to Galway; do supply teaching for a while before getting a permanent job – but he didn't think he could stand it anymore. The pressure, the secrets, the lies he had to use when she couldn't get hold of him on his mobile for a few hours.

No one knew the truth except his counsellor. And it would stay that way. Conor was determined. He just had to stick out this one last trip, to London of all places. He hadn't been since he was a student at university, two decades ago. Land of temptation – perhaps that's why he'd stayed away for so long. Dublin was quite a big place, to be sure, but in London, you could find any type of person you wanted, if you looked hard enough. Sometimes, you didn't even have to look hard at all – they came to you. He should know, after all, especially given what had happened in his final year.

Maybe that was the answer. Maybe he should have stayed in London all those years ago, instead of coming home. He thought he was being the dutiful son, but perhaps he should have put himself first for a change instead of worrying about pleasing everybody else. Plenty of people left Ireland for England and never came back, except for Christmas and the odd weekend. The place of his birth was too claustrophobic, where everyone knew everyone else, and secrets were hard to keep.

The more he thought about it, a plan began to form. Inside the house, he opened the big wardrobe in his bedroom and pulled out a canvas bag from its hiding place behind some sports kit. He chucked a few items into it, locked it with a padlock, then stowed it carefully in the car underneath Mairead's bags.

* * *

The light had faded by the time they'd reached the front of the queue, parked the car in the bowels of the ferry and joined the throng of people who were slowly ascending the stairs to the upper decks. It was Friday night and the ship was packed for the overnight crossing – there were hardly any seats left in the favoured spots of the bar and the self-service restaurant. 'I'm going out for some air,'

Conor announced to Mairead as she was deciding which queue to join first.

'Out there? You're mad, it's freezing so it is.'

'I know but it might settle my stomach. I'm feeling a bit queasy. Must have been that fish and chips.'

'Well, I'm going to buy a magazine and then I'll be in the lounge. I'll save you a seat. See yous later.' Mairead pecked him on the cheek and hurried off to the shop, where a long queue was already forming as passengers equipped themselves for the voyage with newspapers and giant bags of sweets.

There were people packed into almost every corner of the ship – feeding coins into the amusement machines, queueing for coffee, queueing up to buy magazines and snacks in the shop, queueing wherever it was possible to queue. And children everywhere despite the late hour, getting under his feet as they rushed around, treating the ship like a giant playground. One boy barged into him and he resisted the urge to tell him off in his teacher's voice. Mustn't do anything to draw attention to himself.

Near the washrooms, Conor located the door that would let him outside on deck. A fine sea spray was coating everything and he found himself alone, save for another solitary man who was wearing a heavy black overcoat and beanie hat. Both of them gazed out over the choppy, inky black sea, making out the little juddering pinpricks of light that signalled other vessels. A light in the distance flashed on and off – it must be coming from a lighthouse. It looked like the crossing would be rough. *Just my luck*, thought Conor. He wasn't a good traveller at the best of times, and he'd left his seasickness pills at home. What had possessed Mairead to book this crossing? They would have been better off coming over in the summer, when the waters would have been much calmer. He stood there for a few minutes, staring at the horizon, lost in thought, as the other man would recall later when he was questioned by the police.

His fellow passenger glanced at Conor, who had his back turned away, then wrenched open the heavy door and headed back inside. Conor stood on deck for a few more minutes, gazing out to sea, thinking private thoughts. The Irish coast had already disappeared, lost in the fading light and sea mist. His phone screen displayed a message saying that they were now in international waters. He shivered and sighed, the sound immediately lost to the wind. Then he too headed back inside the ship in the direction of the washrooms.

* * *

It was 8 o'clock the next morning and the ship had just docked at the Welsh port of Holyhead, on the Isle of Anglesey. Some passengers had managed to snatch a few hours' sleep overnight but others had stayed up, unable to rest on the choppy crossing. The toilets had been heavily in demand by nauseous passengers and most of them were now blocked by lavatory paper, the floor made dirty and slippery from goodness knows what.

A worried Mairead was speaking to the bored girl perched behind the information desk as the other passengers were streaming past her, heading back to their cars.

'I was only buying a wee magazine,' she said. 'I told him I'd be in the lounge. Yes, of course, I've tried his mobile, but there's no answer. There was no reception out at sea and now it goes straight to voicemail. I've left five messages already. And texts. He said he was feeling sick last night and I'm scared something's happened to him.' She'd already gone to the washrooms and got a passing member of staff to check there was no one left in the gents' cubicles. She hadn't thought of checking the disabled toilet. She'd tried the top restaurant and the bottom restaurant, and even the slot machines, but there was no sign of him.

Meanwhile, everyone else on the ship was on their feet, impatient to be off now that they'd reached Wales, the next step on their onward journeys. The car drivers clattered down the metal steps, back to their vehicles, crammed nose to tail in the hold. Meanwhile, the foot passengers were shuffling forward to the exit, and some, quick off the mark, had disembarked already. They had left the bad weather behind in Ireland, and the sun was starting to rise above the horizon on a still, crisp, windless day.

While Mairead was talking to the ship's young employee, a rather tall, willowy figure in a baseball cap, sunglasses and short leather skirt, carrying a rucksack and canvas bag, looked briefly behind at the disembarking ferry, then briskly headed off on foot in the direction of the bus station in search of an early coach to London, high heels clacking rhythmically on the pavement and a dark brown ponytail swinging under her cap. If you'd troubled to ask her, she might have said in her surprisingly deep voice, 'I used to know a Conor once. But that was a long time ago. I don't think we'll be seeing him again. In fact, I'm certain of it.'

LASTING LEGACY

'There's a tissue in the pocket.'

'As I've already told you, I'd like a refund.'

'And as I've already told *you*, madam, there's a tissue in the pocket. We cannot accept goods back that have been worn.'

'But I only bought this dress on Friday!'

'So I see from the receipt. How do you explain the tissue? And the creasing around the armhole?'

'I—'

'Look, madam, this dress has clearly been worn. I suggest you take it to the dress agency down the road if you have no further use for it. I'm sure they will be more than happy to resell current fashions for you. Minus their commission, of course.'

'How rude!'

With that, the woman snatched up the dress and the receipt, turned around and marched out of the door.

'Or eBay!' shouted Janine after her, feeling annoyed as she closed the door. At least that horrible woman wouldn't come into the shop again. Some people! All that was left of her presence was the offending tissue, bearing a trace of bright pink lipstick, discarded on the glass countertop.

Why did they think she was dim, just because she was a Saturday girl in a dress shop? Or 'boutique' as Sandra, the owner, still liked to call it. Janine was only working there to support herself through her college course. It only paid the minimum wage but what else could she get around here? She was lucky to bag this job, what with all the competition from the other students and people coming over from mainland Europe. It wasn't as if she'd had any retail experience, either. All she'd done before this was a bit of babysitting for her sister. But after Janine had got the job and had been working there for a few weeks, Sandra had confided that she'd mainly employed her because she wanted to take on someone with a 'proper English accent'.

'I know it's not PC, Janine, I'm just saying. People – our ladies – have to understand what comes out of your mouth. It's common sense.'

Janine found she loved working in the shop. You got to meet quite a range of people, considering the town was so small. Sandra was so good at finding flattering clothes for any customer that women travelled from the furthest reaches of Surrey just to hear her advice. They would then spend inordinate amounts of money, or so it seemed to Janine, on entire outfits for special occasions.

Miss O'Keefe, for instance. She was one of Janine's regulars. In her late seventies, perhaps – Janine wasn't too good on ages. Well dressed but rather plump, she would often come in 'just for a browse, sweetie'. She would then become captivated by a particular top and before long would be heard to declare, 'I simply must have it!'

'Never married, no children,' said Sandra, 'and I hear she's not short of a bob or two. Inherited from her father, or so they say. He had his own law firm in the town, practised for years he did. Everybody used to go to him for all their legal affairs before the larger firms muscled in.

'That Miss O'Keefe is a lovely lady, used to be quite a goer from what I've heard, but a bit eccentric… comes of living on her own all this time, if you ask me.'

Janine didn't have a great deal in common with the shop's customers, many of whom were well-heeled Surrey ladies who lunched, including Miss O'Keefe. Still, she found herself liking this particular customer more and more each time she came into the shop. Even if she did have a tendency to stop halfway through a sentence and dash out of the door, exclaiming, 'The meter! It's up!' or gaze out of the shop window and suddenly spot someone she knew, whereupon she would say something like, 'There goes Flo. I simply *must* talk to her about next week's committee meeting,' before flying out of the door.

On one occasion, Miss O'Keefe was actually halfway through typing her PIN number into the machine, having spent a sizeable amount on two jackets and a blouse, when she saw a stray dog outside the shop, skittering from one side of the road to the other.

'Look! The poor little thing! I *must* save it before it's run over.' She rushed out to rescue it while Janine was left holding the blouse in one hand and the PIN machine in the other, with the credit card still protruding from it, wondering if her customer would remember to return. She could see Miss O'Keefe darting down the road after the sizeable black dog. Every now and then she would swoop down to try and grasp hold of its lead, which was trailing along the pavement.

Eventually, a man wearing painting overalls and with heavily tattooed arms appeared from the pub and shouted something, whereupon the dog stopped stock still before trotting back docilely to its owner. Miss O'Keefe advanced upon the man and although Janine couldn't hear what she was saying, she appeared to be telling him off, judging from the jabbing forefinger pointing at his face and the hand on hip.

That day, Miss O'Keefe never did return to finish her transaction, but Janine didn't mind. She wasn't on commission, after all – she was only the Saturday girl – and Miss O'Keefe was still one of the shop's best customers, not to mention one of the more interesting.

Janine liked interacting with the ladies – those who didn't treat her with disdain, anyway. She particularly loved trying to find an item of clothing that would suit the woman in front of her, no matter how skinny or well built she might be, or selling a necklace or scarf that would perfectly complement their chosen purchase. Sandra, of course, loved it when her Saturday girl managed to prize more money from a customer.

Afternoons were always busy but Janine hated the slow mornings when they could go hours between customers, and Sandra would set her to work folding jumpers, checking price tickets or dusting the old-fashioned mannequins in the window display. Sometimes, she was even allowed to dress the mannequins, which had to be subjected to Sandra's strict eye before they could go back in the window. 'It's all about mustard this season, Janine, I want to see mustard accents everywhere. *No!* Not that belt! That belt *will not do*. It will all have to be totally redone.'

One day, Janine's friends from college had come in to say hello but they started fooling about with the clothes. When they started to try on weird combinations for a laugh without any intention of buying anything, she had to shoo them outside before Sandra came back from lunch.

Miss O'Keefe seemed to like Janine. In fact, you could have said that she had rather a soft spot for the youngster. One day, Janine was spending some of her hard-earned money in the café around the corner from the shop. Summer had arrived and it was a hot, sticky afternoon. Most of their usual well-heeled clients seemed to be off playing tennis or topping up tans in their capacious back gardens rather than shopping for clothes. Or maybe they had all swanned off to their second homes in France or Spain. Janine had a hazy idea of what their well off customers got up to in their leisure time. In fact, judging from their conversations with Sandra, the wives did not seem to have to work at all, unless you counted a few hours in the charity shop to 'give something back to the community'. What a life!

Janine was a more down to earth kind of girl. Her mother worked as a mobile hairdresser and her mechanic dad had run off with her mum's best friend when Janine was six, leaving his wife with a four- and two-year-old as well.

'Janine! It *is* you, isn't it? Only my eyes aren't what they used to be and you're not in your usual environment.'

Janine looked up from her phone – it was new, bought with her earnings from the shop. There was Miss O'Keefe, sporting a lurid pink tracksuit, white baseball cap and white pumps.

'I was just out for a nice walk in the sunshine around the park, you know, it's use it or lose it at my age, when I was overtaken by a terrible thirst and I said to myself, "Dora, what you need is an orange, mango and pineapple smoothie from Gilbert's. Nothing else will do." And you dear, is it your lunch hour? *Do* you get a lunch hour or does Sandra normally keep you chained to the shop?'

'I'm on my break, yes,' Janine replied, still goggling at the pink tracksuit and baseball cap. 'To tell the truth, Miss O'Keefe, we haven't had many customers today, what with the sunny weather, so Sandra told me to take my time. I think it's too hot for them to be trying on clothes.'

'Ah, a long lunch break. Jolly good idea,' Miss O'Keefe replied. 'Do call me Dora, dear. All my friends do.' She gazed around the café. 'Do you know, this is my absolutely favourite eatery. I can't be doing with that fancy restaurant they opened in the High Street. And those chain coffee shops, they're too… samey. Full of buggies and toddlers to negotiate around. You can't hear yourself think sometimes, there are so many screaming babies.' Then she seemed to reconsider what she'd said. 'But that's just me, a shrivelled old spinster!' She smiled broadly at her joke. 'Doubtless, you'll be having a family yourself one day, eh dear?'

She changed the subject. 'In fact, I know young Gilbert here very well.' She gestured to the moustachioed owner behind the counter, who caught sight of her and winked. 'We go back a long way, Gilbert and I. A very long way. "Gilbert," I said, "when I'm gone you'll have something to remember me by. A part of me will always be here for the customers to share." Anyway, I mustn't keep you. You'll be wanting to check your phone for messages. I know what you youngsters are like!'

Without waiting for an answer, she was off, bounding out of the door in the direction of the park. All that remained was a waft of something floral and her empty glass. Janine smiled to herself, picked up her phone and prepared to go back to the shop.

* * *

Winter had come early to Cranborough. Janine, now in her second year of college, was still working in the dress shop on Saturdays and sometimes during the week as well, if one of the other staff was on holiday or they were especially busy. Sandra had given her more responsibility and she was now allowed to cash up and lock the shop if her boss had left early for the day. One particularly busy Saturday, she'd had a constant stream of customers almost from when she unlocked the door at 9.30am. It was the party season, in the run-up to Christmas, and Surrey's ladies who lunch were in search of little black dresses, sequinned tops, sparkly cardigans and cropped bolero jackets that would hide the bingo wings on their upper arms.

They would inquire of Janine, 'Has anyone else bought this cardigan? Only it's for the bridge club supper party and I would hate one of the others to be wearing the same thing. So embarrassing.' Janine had to remember who had bought what so as not to annoy her regulars. She joked with Sandra that she needed a database with everyone's clothes purchases on it. Barcodes hadn't even made their way into the shop yet (Sandra was a bit of a traditionalist).

By early afternoon, it was getting dark and in a lull, she made herself a cup of instant coffee. As she snatched a quick sit-down she realised with a start that Miss O'Keefe hadn't been in for several weeks. Not since September, in fact, when she distinctly remembered her favourite customer coming in and announcing she was off on a cruise with her 'gentleman friend'. On that occasion, Miss O'Keefe had bought a smart lilac jacket and patterned scarf, plus a pair of white slacks 'to see me through shore excursions'. The transaction had gone smoothly, she had remembered her PIN number and for once had not been sidetracked by any people, dogs or traffic wardens outside the window. 'Oh, I'm so looking forward to it! I'll send you a postcard at the shop, Janine.'

Janine, who had not received anything in the post, had assumed Miss O'Keefe had simply forgotten. Besides, she must have had plenty of other friends to write to before remembering the shopgirl.

Seeing as there were no customers, she went in search of her boss, who was checking new stock in the back room.

'Sandra, have you seen Miss O'Keefe recently?'

Her boss gave her a funny look. 'Haven't you heard?'

'Heard what?'

'She was taken ill on that cruise. Salmonella or E. coli or something. Lots of them got it. It was in the papers.'

'No, I didn't see anything about it. We don't get the papers at home.'

'Well, according to Candy in the dry cleaners, she was getting worse so they took her off the ship when they got to dry land and put her in some foreign hospital.' (Sandra's tone of voice made it clear what she thought about foreign hospitals.) 'But it was too late.'

'What? What do you mean? Surely, she didn't…?'

'Yes, I'm afraid she did. Passed away. Terribly sad. They brought her body back for cremation. Weren't going to, but she had so much travel insurance, it covered everything. You've no idea what it cost to bring her back. Barry was ever so upset. Blamed himself for suggesting the trip. But it wasn't his fault, of course. How was he to know? Could have happened to anyone on that cruise. Hotbeds of disease they are, I'd never go on one myself.' Sandra gave an involuntary shiver.

'The funeral was last week, I think. After the inquest. No relatives except for a niece. Lots of friends, though. All her bridge cronies, people from all those committees she sat on, probably half our customers. She was ever so popular, was Miss O'Keefe.'

'I never knew…' Janine was shocked. She could hardly believe that Miss O'Keefe ('*Call me Dora, dear, all my friends do*') would never come into the shop again or give a cheery wave to Janine if she saw her on the High Street. Never chase after dogs or flag down traffic wardens to distract them from ticketing someone she knew.

Sandra put her arm round Janine. 'I know you had a soft spot for her, Janine, love, and I think she had one for you. You talk to Gilbert in the café. He'll tell you more about her. My goodness, he's got some tales to tell.'

* * *

A few days later, Janine was in the coffee shop again for a late lunch. She was feeling a bit down and decided to treat herself. It was the first chance she'd had to go in for a while, the shop having been so busy. She normally went in once a week to get a takeaway coffee on her way home from the shop, and sometimes grabbed a sandwich there at lunchtime too. The café owner grinned at her and said, 'Ooh you haven't been in for a while. Can I tempt you with one of my new special coffees? They're delicious, even if I say so myself.'

'That would be lovely,' Janine replied. She looked around the counter, with its tempting display of huge sponge cakes and traybakes, while behind Gilbert there were tall jars containing marshmallows, chocolate flakes, sprinkles, cocoa powder and a couple of ingredients she couldn't identify.

'I'll bring it over to you,' came Gilbert's voice from behind the industrial looking coffee machine.

Janine went over to her favourite spot by the window, a table for two. For once, the café was almost deserted, as lunch had now finished and there was still some time to go before the four o'clock rush. She took out her phone and started reading her texts. She had been going to talk to Gilbert about Miss O'Keefe but wasn't sure she could face it now. Thinking about her still brought tears to her eyes.

The drink smelt delicious. Janine wasn't a coffee connoisseur but she needed the caffeine after a tiring day on her feet in the shop. This one was extra strong, just how she liked it, with three shots of espresso. She could feel a cold coming on, which meant it took a while for her taste buds to detect something else in the steaming drink. It had almost a grainy texture that even gave it a bit of a kick… she couldn't put her finger on exactly what it was.

'Miss Dora, do you?' said a voice. Gilbert was standing at the next table, wiping it down.

'Oh yes,' said Janine, putting her phone down. 'Yes, I do. She used to come into the shop quite often. I like Sandra a lot, of course, but it won't be the same without Miss O'Keefe.'

'I know exactly what you mean,' said Gilbert. 'She was one of my best customers. Not just for drinks. She had lunch or afternoon tea here more than once a week. I think she was lonely.' He saw the expression of surprise on Janine's face. 'Oh I know, she had lots of friends in the bridge club and that, but she was still lonely. No partner, no one at home to talk to – except the cleaner and the gardener, of course. Money can't buy you everything. "Gilbert," she said to me once, "Gilbert, you won't forget me, will you?" Of course, I won't,' I said. "How could I forget you? You'll see me out, you will, even though I'm ten years younger than you." He let out a heavy sigh. 'I was proved wrong there, wasn't I?

'Well, just before she went on that cruise with her friend Barry – oh, he wasn't a boyfriend, nothing like that, just an old acquaintance of hers from her golfing days – I think she had a sort of premonition. That something might happen. God knows why. I mean, she used to travel all over the place. China, Vietnam, Russia, the Caribbean… you name it, she'd been there. This was only a Mediterranean cruise, for goodness sake!

'Anyway, about a week before she set off, she came in to see me and said she'd rewritten her will. Said I'd get a little present if anything happened to her but it wasn't going to be money, or anything valuable, and I was to think no more about it unless the day ever came. Said it was meant for her favourite customers in this café. She used to chat to quite a few, you see. That's partly why she came in so often. I'm sure it wasn't just for my cakes, delicious though they are.

'So I put it out of my mind until the other day, when this man appeared with a package. I knew she'd died but he said it was from Miss O'Keefe herself, with instructions that it was to be shared among her friends. So I thought of you and a couple of others. Dora often mentioned you, you know.'

Janine had been listening with interest to Gilbert but in the last few moments had begun to get a worrying feeling in her stomach, to go with the tingling in the back of her throat. Thoughts started to whirl around in her head. Present… Miss O'Keefe… cremation… something to remember her by… The strange taste in her mouth seemed to crystallise into something definitely *not* edible and she fought a sudden urge to gag.

She spat out her drink and looked wildly around for water. 'Gilbert. *Gilbert!*' she said urgently. 'You're not going to tell me what I think you are. Tell me you didn't add something to that drink.'

'Add something? Well, yes I did, as it happens. Don't you like it? Only—'

'What exactly did you add, Gilbert?' A terrible vision had just come into Janine's mind. A vision of Miss O'Keefe's funeral. Cremation, Sandra had said. Cremation means ashes. The man with the package… Had the ashes, instead of being stored in an urn or interred in a cemetery, found their way into one of the mysterious glass jars behind Gilbert's counter? Could he have unknowingly sprinkled them into customers' drinks to make a 'special' concoction? *Her* drink? Was she even now drinking Miss O'Keefe's remains…?

God. Surely not. But the woman *had* been a bit mad, after all. Nice enough but a little… scatty.

Another moment and she'd be sick, she was sure of it. The more she thought about what she might have drunk, the sicker she felt. In fact – she flung her bag aside, got up and bolted to the ladies just in time, trying to retch quietly into the bowl so that Gilbert wouldn't realise.

It was over as quickly as it had started. Nothing more to come up, thank goodness. She flushed the toilet, wiped her face with a paper towel, swilled some water from the tap round her mouth to try and get rid of the smell, and looked in the mirror. She checked that she looked more or less presentable, then made her way back to the table. Gilbert was staring at her, mouth open, a worried expression on his face.

'Lucky you're the only customer here,' he said. 'Otherwise, everybody else would have walked out after they saw what my drink did to you. I added a bit more than the packet said, but still…'

'Sorry?'

'Ginger. What I added to the drink,' he said.

'Ginger?' The one food she took pains to avoid, on account of the reaction she'd had to it the previous year. 'Oh Gilbert, you'll think I'm so stupid…'

'Just wanted to give it a little kick, that's all. Only…' he looked at Janine with a sheepish smile, 'it seems I'd better add a little less next time. Thank you for being my first tester. Your next order's on the house!'

He started heading back to the counter, cloth in hand, then turned back. 'Oh yes. That parcel from Miss O'Keefe. Isn't it magnificent? Now we can look at that and all remember her. She was quite a beauty when she was younger.'

Janine followed his gaze. Gilbert's café had several mismatched pictures on the walls, all in wonky frames – it was partly what gave it its appealing character. Hanging up behind the counter, next to the old-fashioned clock, was one she hadn't noticed before. It was in an ornate gilt frame and showed a study in oils of a young woman in tennis whites, holding a racquet, her head slightly inclined, her expression impish, as if she had just said something cheeky to the artist. The woman was probably around twenty-five years old, not much older than Janine, fresh-faced with a cascade of blonde curls and incredibly slim. It was, however, undoubtedly Miss Dora O'Keefe.

FINDERS KEEPERS

'Mum.'

I was still thinking about Jed, too busy to pay attention to my own son.

'Mummee.'

'Mum!' The voice was getting louder, more insistent.

'What is it?' I tried to keep the irritation out of my voice.

'Can I have an ice cream?'

'No. Not today.'

'But that boy over there is having one. Look! Can I have one too? Can I? Plee-ease?'

The precise, persistent reasoning of an eight-year-old, who would never understand the real reason why his mummy didn't want him to have an ice cream. Who would just think she was being mean or worrying about his teeth again. I changed the subject rapidly.

'Shall we go to the playground? It says here that there's an outdoor adventure trail. That sounds fun.'

'Mum, I want an ice cream. Now.'

'Wait 'til we get home and you can have a lolly from the freezer.'

'But I want one *now*.'

'I said no and that's an end to it.' I was trying to keep my voice under control, aware of the looks in our direction from other visitors.

Feeling a meltdown was about to come on, I frogmarched my son to the play area. Visiting this place had seemed like a good idea two hours ago. It was the school holidays and I was struggling to think of suitable things to do with Ethan. By 'suitable', I really mean cheap. I didn't work and Jed, his dad, had moved out six months earlier. The money he'd promised me, the monthly payment so that I could buy essentials like school uniform and shoes, which Ethan was forever growing out of, still hadn't materialised. So we had no spare funds for treats, not even for things like ice cream.

Then, seemingly out of nowhere, the summer holidays had arrived. Six whole weeks to fill. When Jed was around, we'd had a fortnight at the seaside every summer – Dorset or Devon usually; even talked about camping in the South of France, but that was out of the question now. We'd exhausted the possibilities of the park and the playground around the corner, and I was getting desperate for things to do which wouldn't involve money. Friends had been good and invited us out on picnics or bike rides, but after three weeks, everyone I knew seemed to have departed for their annual trips to the West Country, Spain or Greece, or deposited their children with the grandparents. We, of course, were staying at home. My own parents were long dead and relations with Jed's parents were strained, to put it mildly, seeing as how they thought that I was entirely to blame for him walking out. I desperately needed some adult company. Or at least, to be in a place where there were some other adults and I could immerse myself in some adult conversation.

Then, as I was going through the contents of my purse to weed out old receipts and expired money-off vouchers, I spotted a season ticket to the local stately home lurking behind my library card. I'd applied for it months ago in a fit of enthusiasm, when we still had money and the three of us used to go out at the weekend, exploring. We'd take our bikes to the forest, ride the long trails around the lake and finish up in the café, which was trickier now that I didn't have a car. Or we'd go to theme parks and I'd be terrified on the rides, while Jed and Ethan loved the thrills of the rollercoaster and the watersplash.

That was before the rows, before Jed's long absences and then, finally, him walking out one night and never coming back, save to pick up his things. Ethan still saw him from time to time, but never at our home – I would drive my son to meet his father on neutral territory, at least when the car was still working.

Today, though, I had resolved not to think about Jed.

'Ethan, would you like to go somewhere exciting?'

What with Jed leaving, we had never actually been to Downscott Manor despite me buying the season ticket, although we'd often talked about it. It didn't take long to catch the bus to the village and then we walked the rest of the way. Still in private hands, the Manor was a grand, symmetrical house standing imposingly at the end of a mile-long drive lined with lime trees. Just as we were walking along it, the sun came out and filtered down through the branches, throwing pleasing patterns on the track. *What a glorious place*, I thought as we came upon the house itself, with its honey-coloured stone, mullioned windows and imposing arched entrance flanked by two huge stone lions.

I couldn't afford the guidebook but I'd printed off some information from the Internet before we'd set off, and I wanted to see the interior of the house, which had been owned by a well to do gentleman in the 1800s. Ethan, however, had other ideas. He insisted on seeing the pets' graveyard which I'd rashly mentioned on the way there. 'Are they all buried under the earth, Mummy? What happens to dogs and cats when they die? Do they go to dog and cat heaven? Can we get a dog?'

I sighed inwardly. The last thing we needed right now was a pet, what with the cost of food and all the vets' bills. 'Come on, let's find the adventure trail.' Ethan charged off, all thoughts of a pet forgotten. For now, anyway. A 'natural playground', mainly consisting of tree trunks ingeniously fashioned into an assault course, was set in a clearing away from the house and manicured lawn, where many families were picnicking on blankets to the sound of jazz music from a quartet.

In the woods, Ethan patiently waited his turn while other children navigated the course, some gingerly, some expertly. When it was his turn he managed to get around without touching the ground once. He jumped off triumphantly and shouted, 'Done it! Can I have another go?'

I was content to perch on a log in the dappled sunlight while I waited for him, watching the other families having fun. I was used to being on my own now. There were one or two solitary dads who looked like they could have been having their children just for the weekend, before handing them back. These were the ones who tended to overcompensate for everything. When their kids were bought ice creams they would be the biggest one imaginable, triple scoops dripping with chocolate sauce, lurid sprinkles and a flake. When these children were going around the assault course, the dads would urge them on, shouting something like, 'Come on! You can do better than that!' Doubtless, they would be bought lots of souvenirs in the shop too, to ensure they had good memories of the day out, before being deposited back at the ex-partner's.

I tried not to feel bitter about Jed but it was hard, so hard. I couldn't bad mouth him in front of Ethan but some evenings, when my son was playing up and I was tired, I just wished there was another adult in the house to back me up or who could take over for a while. Here though, in the grounds of this lovely stately home, I felt more at peace than I had done for months.

You don't have to do it all, said a voice in my head. *Just concentrate on being the best mother you can be to your son. Don't waste your life waiting for Jed to come back because you know he won't. It's just you and Ethan now.*

Ethan was coming towards me, the knees of his jeans, and his hands, covered in mud but with a big grin on his face. 'That was awesome, Mum! Can we come here again?'

'Yes, of course. I've got a season ticket now. Fancy checking out the bird hide? See if we can spot anything rare? You'll have to be really quiet so you don't scare the birds!'

We set off in search of the hide, from where you could see birds eating nuts from a feeder suspended from a tree. There was no one else watching the birds. On a blackboard, people had written down the species they had spotted that day. At least, I could tell myself that it was educational for Ethan. I was happily watching a tiny wren carefully extracting a nut when he said, 'Look, Mum, look what I found.'

I turned to see him holding up a battered, bulging leather wallet. Someone must have dropped it while they were engrossed in birdwatching, but the hide was now empty, save for us.

Before I could stop him, Ethan unfolded the wallet. 'Wow! Mum! Look! Look how much money there is!'

He carefully extracted a wad of notes, then held them up in a fan to show me. It was like one of those '80s game shows. They were all £50 denomination. There must have been at least twenty there. Fifty times twenty… I did a quick sum. That would be a thousand pounds! I couldn't recall seeing a £50 note before but they all had the silver line running through them and they looked genuine enough. A thousand pounds… that would pay all our bills for a while. Or Ethan's school clubs and uniform and shoes, with enough for a little holiday as well… Or perhaps an old banger so that we had our own transport again. Or…

I glanced around. There was still nobody about. Everyone was at the playground or on the lawn, relaxing to the music which you could just hear from where we were. It would be so easy to pocket the cash, with nobody knowing. We could leave the wallet where it was, or take it and throw it away later. God knows, we could really do with the money. On the other hand, the money wasn't ours. Somebody would be missing it. If not now, then later. Anyway, what if someone saw us taking it?

'Is there anything else in the wallet, Ethan?'

'Like what?'

'A name?'

If there was any sort of ID in there, I'd feel compelled to return it to the rightful owner. Otherwise, I'd just feel guilty for days.

'Nope. No name. No credit cards. Just a receipt. Can I keep it, Mum? Can I? Then I can buy that Lego spaceship, the same one as Daniel's got.'

'Hold on a moment. Give me that receipt please.' Did it have a credit card number on it? No, it was for cash and it didn't even have the name of the shop on it. So no means of identifying the purchaser.

I held out my hand for the wallet. Ethan reluctantly gave it to me. I turned it over in my hand, several times, while I thought what to do for the best. It was perfectly dry and clean so someone had probably only just dropped it. Should I ask at the play area? I glanced around. There was still no one about. Should we keep the money? I was tempted, so tempted. It would go against all the values I'd tried to instil in my son, not to mention my own values. Turning it around, what if I had been the one to lose my own purse? I would be devastated if it never turned up. Then again, who would be so stupid as to walk around with that much money in their pocket? Perhaps it belonged to a drug dealer. Someone up to no good. A criminal who didn't deserve the cash. On the other hand, maybe someone had just paid their builder in cash? You couldn't blame them, these days, wanting to save on tax.

I gazed at the distant fields, where you could make out a few cows grazing on the upper slopes. Then I came to a decision.

'No. We have to hand it in at the desk. We'll just go back to the play area first, check that no one there owns it. There's a lot of money in there and whoever dropped that wallet will be desperate to have it back. They probably had so much in there for a special reason. Something they'd saved up to buy, perhaps. Let's go.'

A painful expression fleetingly passed across Ethan's face – no doubt thinking about the Lego set he could have had. But then, it was gone and he was haring off again, back the way we'd come, his mind already on other things.

* * *

The elderly volunteer in an equally elderly cord jacket who was manning the entrance desk thanked me profusely when I handed in the wallet, explaining where we'd found it. 'Oh, thank you so much, madam, it's nice to know there are still honest people about.' He unfolded it and his eyes widened. 'My goodness! What a lot of cash! Maybe he was about to buy a second-hand car, eh? Or did he rob a bank?' He winked at Ethan.

'Well, madam, we'll keep it safely under lock and key and see if we can track down the owner. It's nearly closing time, so he – or she – could well have left by now, but perhaps we'll put out a message on social media.' He cleared his throat. 'Not me you understand, but one of the young ladies in our marketing department will know how to do it, I'm sure. And I'll tell our Mr Broadbent that you came in – he's lord of the manor, as I call him. Likes to be kept in touch with what's going on. Perhaps there'll be a reward, eh?' He winked at me.

I hadn't thought of that. I left my name and mobile number with the volunteer and when we started for home, I was in a good mood again.

* * *

September

It seemed like ages since we'd visited Downscott Manor. I'd meant to go back that summer but in the end, the time flew by. Ethan discovered the new skate park and there was no stopping him. He must have been the youngest there but he loved to whizz up and down the ramps and attempt tricks like the older ones. I made him wear elbow pads and long sleeves and, thankfully, he came to no real harm, just a couple of tumbles and some grazed knuckles. I would sit and watch him, not going into the café to buy an overpriced cappuccino, but bringing along my own coffee in an insulated mug to save money. It just felt good knowing that Ethan was happy and occupied for free while I was sitting in the sunshine. Sometimes, if I wasn't reading a library book, I would chat with the other parents.

Actually, I'd almost forgotten about our visit to the Manor. They'd never rung me back so I assumed the wallet had been handed back to someone who didn't wish to give me a reward. I couldn't believe that no one had claimed it. You wouldn't just forget about a thing like that. It was disappointing, but I knew I'd done the right thing handing it in. If I'd kept the money, it would have been on my conscience for evermore. Ethan, thankfully, seemed to have forgotten all about his find. In any case, now he was back at school he had friends, clubs and playdates more on his mind. I was trying to get him to focus on his schoolwork but he just wanted to enjoy himself.

Since I had more spare time now, I was pressing on with my quest to find some part-time work which would fit around Ethan's holidays. It was proving difficult, especially since we had no grandparents or other close family who might be able to help out. The after-school club was full and private childcare was far too expensive. My friends were all busy with their own concerns, juggling childcare with jobs and family commitments. Jed hadn't even bothered to call to find out how the new class was going. I had a text saying he'd take Ethan to the cinema that weekend, but that was it.

Then, one day, as I was making a sandwich for lunch my mobile rang from the depths of my bag. It said, 'Number withheld,' which usually meant someone was trying to sell me something, but I answered anyway, just in case it was important. A rather posh voice said, 'Is that Miss Warnes?' Would you believe, it turned out to be Mr Broadbent himself from Downscott Manor! He sounded older and had that plummy accent you don't often hear nowadays. Like the one the Queen used to have when she was younger, before she had to tone it down. He thanked me profusely, as the volunteer had done, and said that the wallet had finally been restored to its rightful owner, who was most grateful. He didn't give any more details and I didn't like to ask. I wanted to find out how the man (I assumed it was a man, seeing as it had been a man's wallet) had come by the money but didn't want to sound too inquisitive. The mystery would have to stay just that.

I didn't like to ask about the possibility of a reward, either, but as if reading my mind, Mr Broadbent said, 'I'm afraid the gentleman left in a hurry without leaving any money for the finder, and as a charity, we don't have the funds to reward people ourselves. Things turn up all the time – you'd be astonished at what people leave behind here, it's as bad as the London Underground. Although I must say, we haven't had anything as valuable as that wallet before. I'm sure you'll understand.'

That was that, then.

'Oh, of course, I do understand,' I murmured, trying not to let the disappointment show in my voice, but he was still talking.

'However, as some sort of recognition for your noble actions, I'd be delighted to treat you to lunch at Downscott Hall. You and your family. How does that sound?'

'Well…' I didn't know what to say. 'It's really very generous, Mr Broadbent, but quite unnecessary.'

'Nevertheless, I should like to treat you to the finest fare from our restaurant. Ernest, my volunteer, tells me that you have a young son? You can tell him that we specialise in very fine ice creams. I am particularly fond of the pistachio. Do bring your partner too. Shall we say Sunday? About noon? Just ask for me at the entrance.'

'Well, I… Yes, yes of course. Thank you so much.'

He rang off. I was in a bit of a daze. A free lunch at Downscott Manor! I'd never tried it, of course, but I had heard from my neighbour that the food was excellent. It would be our unexpected weekend treat.

So that Sunday Ethan and I found ourselves back at the Manor, sitting down to a three-course meal in the rather smart restaurant. No self-service bunfight here. Not only that, but Mr Broadbent himself joined us. He was in his late sixties, I'd guess, still with a full head of very dark, almost black hair (no stranger to hair dye, surely), beaten into submission by some sort of hair gel, and heavy, plastic-framed spectacles perched on the end of his nose. He was wearing a tweed jacket and red cord trousers – red! – with polished tan brogues and a handkerchief poking out of his breast pocket. *The upper classes are alive and well*, I thought to myself. I'd smartened myself up a bit and made Ethan wear his one respectable shirt. It felt a bit awkward at first but I gradually loosened up and we began chatting. Ethan was happy to tuck into the biggest meal he'd had for months.

I'd been worried about taking him somewhere 'posh' when the only restaurant we ventured into was the local pizza place (and I couldn't afford that very often now), but so far he was behaving impeccably.

Downscott Manor's owner ('Well, I'm more of the custodian actually') asked me how often I visited. 'Well, when we found the wallet, it was our first time,' I found myself admitting. 'It's just the two of us, me and Ethan, and sometimes it's quite tricky to get to places.' I didn't mention that we never went anywhere because I always had to watch what I spent. 'Now I have a membership card, though, I'm sure we'll be coming here more often.'

'I see. And do you work, Miss Warnes?'

'Not at the moment, no. I like to be around for Ethan when he's not in school, and it's a bit difficult to find childcare at the moment… I trailed off.'

'Hmmm.' Mr Broadbent seemed to be considering something. He picked up the rather large, heavy looking salt cellar. 'I've never liked these. Must ask them to order different ones.'

Then, he suddenly stood up and made to shake my hand. 'Well, it's been lovely meeting you, and your delightful son. I'm afraid I'm late for a meeting, please excuse me. Take as long as you like, both of you. Everything's on the house, as they say.' Ethan had, thankfully, stayed quiet for a change, and was now about to tuck into a huge chocolate ice cream sundae festooned with wafers and chocolate buttons. His eyes had nearly been out on stalks when it was ceremoniously placed in front of him by the waitress.

'Just one thing before I go. You'll be pleased to hear you've passed the interview, Miss Warnes.'

'Sorry?'

'For the job. Didn't they tell you?'

'Err…'

'I'm looking for someone who can be my assistant. Not working in the kitchens or serving at the table or anything like that, my goodness no. We leave that to the teenagers. The thing is, I need someone to be my personal assistant. Doing a bit of marketing – selling the old place to visitors, increasing their numbers, especially in the winter, that kind of thing. Bit of admin – not my strongest point, I'm afraid. You did mention you had a marketing background, did you not? It should be right up your street. The main quality I'm looking for, though, is honesty. My last assistant was a bit, shall we say, *careless* with the finances.

'Well, you've most certainly proved you're honest to the core by handing in that wallet. A lot of people would have pocketed the cash and never said a word. I happen to know that not one banknote was missing. Now, what do you say? Yes or no?'

'Well…'

I was amazed. I hadn't seen that coming. How could I turn him down politely?

'Err, it's all a bit sudden. Thank you very much for considering me. It's a lovely job, I'm sure, and it's true that I *am* looking for employment at the moment, but I don't think I'm the right candidate.'

'Why ever not?'

'Well, the thing is, I can't work full-time because of Ethan. Picking him up from school, then there are the holidays to think of…'

'No problem at all. I'd anticipated that. I may not have children myself, but I'm not quite the old fogey I seem,' he said, with a crafty smile on his face. 'I'll have you know I have three Godchildren.'

'You can work the hours you want. If we need help during the busy summer season, I can always get Deirdre from the office to muck in. She's quite used to it. I've been relying on her since my previous assistant – ah – decided it best if she left. And if we do find you indispensable during the holidays, I'm sure young Ethan here could be entertained in some way… do you like horse riding, young man? There's a stable on the estate, you know. Jim who works there could do with a helper, I'm sure. If you don't mind mucking out…'

Ethan paused to look up from eating his ice cream, his face (now rather mucky) beaming. He loved horses, only the nearest he'd come to a ride on one was five minutes around the sports field at the school fair. Of course, I'd never thought of treating him to riding lessons because of the huge expense.

Mr Broadbent had taken me completely by surprise. It was all rather overwhelming.

'I don't know what to say, Mr Broadbent…'

'Do call me Rupert. Have a think, Miss Warnes. We're pretty informal here when it comes to job offers. None of that Human Resources nonsense. References are a waste of time, in my experience. And CVs. Gut feeling, that's what I go on. Never let me down. Should have listened to it when I took on my last assistant, but we were so desperate for help, I let myself be persuaded by other people. And look where it got me!

'But enough of that. Do let me know by the end of the week. Lovely to meet you and I'll be in touch. Goodbye!' With that, he jumped up with surprising speed and set off in the direction of the shop.

'Mum! What was he saying about a job? I think you should take it. I get to ride horses! And you'll still be able to pick me up. Mum!'

I looked at my son, who was carefully transferring the chocolate smeared all over his face to the snow white linen napkin, and smiled. Finding the wallet had turned out OK, after all. After all that had happened with Jed, I was due some luck, and here it was. Things were going to get better from here, I was sure of it.

Acknowledgements

With thanks to Leonora Meriel, whose publishing journey inspired my own; my two reading groups, for their friendship, chat and laughter; Leila Green for helping me get my book off the ground; first readers Linda Haydon, Katie Keith, Nadia McGoff and Jeanie Murray for their helpful comments pre-publication; Tim Russell for going through the text with a fine-tooth comb; Ravina Patel for the wonderful cover design; for their enthusiasm and encouragement, my Wednesday morning coffee companions (ladies – you know who you are). All errors are, of course, my own.

The author

Sarah Boyd has a background in magazine publishing and journalism. This is her first book. She lives in South West London with her family and is currently working on her second collection of short stories.

29799204R00149

Printed in Great
Britain
by Amazon